Cloudbusting

Slade Roberson
5632 Shady Branch Dr
Chattanooga, TN 37415
www.sladeroberson.com

This is a work of fiction. Names, characters, places, and
incidents are a product of the author's imagination or are
used fictitiously. Locales and public names are sometimes
used for atmospheric purposes. Any resemblance to actual
persons, living or dead, or to businesses establishments,
events, institutions, or locales is completely coincidental.
cover image dotlizard via Creative Commons | Flickr
CC BY-SA 2.0

Cloudbusting/ Slade Roberson. — 1st ed.
ISBN 978-0-9916523-0-3 (pb)

Cloudbusting

a novella

Slade Roberson

ONE

Charlotte wasn't the only person I'd ever met who claimed she could control the weather, but she was the first to make it rain right in front of me while she talked me through the process.

Of all the storms that summer, there were a few that I could personally attribute to her magic: two that qualified as afternoon thundershowers and another of a significantly more dangerous form, which, to keep things simple, I'd call a *tornado*. And I'm fairly convinced I had at least co-authored that one.

I met Charlotte in July 1988, between my freshman and sophomore years in college. She was dating a friend of mine named Mickey, known by most people as the guy who sold us acid. Mickey called me one sweltering afternoon and asked me to come pick him up and give him a ride. I hadn't heard from him in about six weeks, which was unusual.

When I got downtown, I did a slow crawl through College Square, but I didn't see Mickey anywhere. I drove around the block a few times, but thankfully, just before I was about to repeat the cycle, a truck pulled out of a space in front of the Cookies & Company Café. Surely he wouldn't miss me parked right there on one of the main corners in a big old sky-blue Mercedes.

I rolled down the windows before I cut the engine; at this point in the year, the car's ancient air conditioner was nothing more than a symbolic gesture. A drop of sweat ran straight down my chest and pooled in my navel. Behind my sunglasses I watched a group of pretty townie guys sitting at their regular outdoor table by the café and looking over my way, muttering to one another. They all smiled at once, clearly talking about me or my car or both. I wondered who came up with the name Freon and if it was something I could add to the vehicle myself.

Mickey came from out of nowhere, threw himself inside, slammed the passenger door, and grinned at me. "Brother, you are going to be so glad you did me this favor."

"Oh, yeah?" I asked. "Why is that?" It wasn't exactly a real question, more of a polite script. Mickey's grin usually had something to do with whatever drugs he'd most recently obtained. To his credit, his enthusiasm wasn't just salesmanship; he was genuinely excited about his product.

"Wait'll you see this." He started rooting around in his army surplus satchel.

I cranked the engine, angled one of the air vents to blow on Mickey, and hopefully adjusted the others at my own face. "Put your seat belt on, man."

He ignored me. "Check it out." He held his hand out low and close to the dashboard stereo controls. I glanced down at an open fold of aluminum foil on his palm. Nestled in the crease was a brand-new sheet of blotter acid: a white rectangle of paper printed with tiny, repeating red images in perforated rows like a toy book of stamps. It always struck me as a whimsical form for a drug—itty-bitty cartoons on paper that you stuck on your tongue and poisoned yourself with. "Not just regular blotter, either," Mickey said. "Double dipped. Every hit has multiple drops of pure liquid LSD."

"Multiple, huh?" I put my right hand on the headrest behind him and twisted around in my seat to watch for a break in traffic.

"Yeah, like, at least two."

"That's usually what double means," I said, backing out.

Mickey cackled. He had no problem laughing at himself.

I drove around the block one more time to get back on Broad Street and immediately caught the light in front of the Arches. A stream of pedestrians crossed the walk at the main entrance to Old Campus. While we were stopped, I squinted down at the blotter balanced on Mickey's knee, trying to make out the miniature graphics. "What the hell are those supposed to be?"

"Hearts. With little white clock faces in the center,"

Mickey said, arching an eyebrow. "It's called Tin Woodman." He looked as proud as if he'd come up with the concept himself.

I stared at him for a moment with my mouth hanging open. "No way," I said.

"I know, isn't that killer?" He mistook my reaction for being impressed.

The light turned green, and I accelerated away from town. "Man..." I said, shaking my head. "Look in the glove compartment."

Mickey fumbled with the release, the tin foil of LSD tipping precariously and sliding toward the floorboard.

"And put those away," I said through clenched teeth. "There's a cop right behind us."

With his left hand, he stashed the drugs in the bag between his feet, and with his right, he caught the postcard that fluttered out of the glove compartment when the door dropped open.

"That's it," I said. "You don't have to *read* it, though. Just look at the picture."

He flipped it over, immediately taking in the illustration of the Tin Woodman from the original book version of *The Wizard of Oz*. "No fucking way," Mickey breathed in a loud stage whisper.

"That's what I'm saying," I said.

"I have chills." He shuddered dramatically, rubbing his arm above the elbow.

I held out my own arm so he could see the goosebumps.

"When did you get this?" he asked, already turning the postcard over and reading it anyway. "It's from Hutch. Where the hell is he?" I wondered if Mickey had actually noticed that there was no return address.

"Somewhere in New York." I'm sure I made it sound like one of the most disgusting places on earth. "Brooklyn, maybe?"

"You guys were supposed to get a place together for the summer," Mickey said, his mouth twisted in exaggerated confusion.

"Indeed we were," I said. Hutch was one of Mickey's best friends, and even though it wasn't talked about in any kind of official way yet, it had to be pretty obvious, to anyone who knew both of us, that Hutch and I were, like, *together*. Or headed that way. "He got a better offer."

"From who?" Mickey asked, like he couldn't fathom it.

"That guy from high school he always talks about. *William*."

There was no need to say much else. I didn't feel like going into a lot of detail about how I'd been abandoned in Athens for the summer. I had miscalculated all my friendships, really. I thought everybody would want to hang out in town for a few months without any classes to keep up with—just work some shitty part-time jobs and go out. Most of my friends' families were only an hour away in Atlanta. They'd all surprised me by reaching backward for lightened responsibilities: resurrecting the minimum-wage counter services they'd perfected in high school, partying with old friends they no longer had that much in common with, enjoying unlimited coin-less laundry and refrigerators they didn't have to stock, and catching up on the cable TV they'd forgotten existed. All from bedrooms at their parents' houses that they didn't have to share or pay for.

"Where are you living then?" Mickey asked, reaching for one of my cigarettes without asking. He had adopted the local custom of hand-rolling his own smokes, but he bummed pre-rolls whenever that became inconvenient.

I caught him up on how I'd had to lease a two-bedroom apartment with three other guys who had lived on my hall in Reed during our freshman year. The inappropriately named College Center Apartments. It was one of those cracker box university complexes that are basically hotel-sized dorms so ridiculously far from any part of campus—much less the center—that you absolutely had to have a car. Then you were constantly late for classes every morning, driving around trying to find somewhere to park. My big blue tank kept me from squeezing into the kinds of inventive spaces that the drivers of Honda Civic hatchbacks took for granted. The practicality of all that was admittedly indefensible, but the status of living off campus was worth quite a bit.

My roommates all had girlfriends who were always at the apartment hanging out or sleeping over. The six of them spent a lot of time behind a coffee-table pyramid of PBR cans and Genesee bottles, their gatherings accompanied by ceaseless loud television and the cackling bray of the newly alcoholic. I stayed away as much as possible. I kept my clothes there along with a futon mattress, a banker's lamp, and an alarm clock on the floor. I worried about the effectiveness of the two padlocked camp trunks in the closet where I'd stashed my music collection. When I wasn't working my retail job, the only person from our crowd who'd stayed in town that I felt comfortable hanging out with was our drug dealer, Mickey.

I'm sure he could tell from my silence that the subject needed to be changed again.

"So, I guess you're working somewhere," he said.

I pulled into the turn lane to take a left onto Milledge and got caught by yet another light. I looked over at him and pointedly rolled my eyes. "Macy's, out at the mall. I'm a sales associate in the Ralph Lauren Polo shop."

He grimaced sympathetically. "You should apply at the Gap. They're going to open a store right down in the square. You know that Paul Revere–looking dude? He's a manager, and he buys—"

I was already shaking my head before he could finish. "I tried. They hire all their friends to work there. He was nice enough—I think he actually tried not to be too condescending—but he basically told me I'd have to spend most of my paycheck on a bunch of new Gap clothes. You have to wear their shit. Like, current stuff."

"Ugh."

I got a green turn arrow and floored the gas a little too much.

"Yeah, it's bad when you're too preppy for the Gap," I said. "He did me a favor, though. The Polo shop? I've got a closet full of that shit from high school. I can roll out of bed looking like that, even hung over. I was hung over during the interview."

"You're just one of those people who always looks fresh and pressed," Mickey said. "It's like a magic power. Clean-cut camouflage or something."

"Fuck you," I said, with genuine affection.

We sat through another couple of blocks and another red light without talking.

"Brother, this," he said, waving the postcard at me, "is a sign."

"A sign? Of what?"

"A sign that you should sample the blood of the Tin Woodman's heart with me. Come over to Charlotte's. I talk about you all the time. She's really cool. Her place is amazing."

Whenever he began to say her name—the phonetic *sh*—for a fraction of a second I couldn't help but think he was going to call her "Sugar." I'd almost forget her real name, and then every once in a while he'd say it.

Those who had met her called her Sugar behind her back because that was what she called everybody else to their faces. They never got tired of impersonating her Old South pretensions, chief among them, "Oh, Sugar!" Later, I found it was true; she began nearly every sentence with it. Never "Darlin' " and certainly not "Honey." No. *Sugar.*

Mickey was basically living with Charlotte. She leased one of the singularly most coveted apartments in all of town, one of only two end units on the top floor of a three-story 1920s building owned by Stein Properties. It had a screened porch that looked over a corner wedge of trees and a sidewalk that reached out into the Five Points intersection of South Lumpkin Street, South Milledge Avenue, and Milledge Circle.

Before he'd met Charlotte—before he'd even officially moved out of the dorms—Mickey started crashing at the Commune a few blocks down South Lumpkin, just past Hope Avenue. The Commune was a block of adjacent houses that appeared to be perfectly gentrified 1930s bungalows but that were actually the best-known non-Greek party houses in town—and the worst-kept secret in marijuana distribution.

We would sit at that Five Points intersection, coming and going on procurement errands to and from the Commune or pulling in and out of the Five Points Bottle Shop parking lot, and we'd look up and marvel out loud at the prize that was that one particular apartment.

Charlotte's apartment, it turned out.

Mickey showed me where I could park in the lot behind the row of shops adjacent to her building. There was a space-that-wasn't-a-space behind a fenced-off Dumpster.

We trudged around to a side entrance I'd never noticed before between a pair of enormous magnolia trees. The weather was that kind of hot where the air didn't move, and the sky was whiter than it was blue.

I heard a voice call, "Hey, Sugar!" We looked up to see a wide, foreshortened smile framed by a dark flapper bob swinging out a third-story window. "Will y'all run over to the Bottle Shop and get me a carton of cigarettes?"

Something hit the sidewalk. Mickey dove to catch it but missed. I flinched, not knowing what it was until he scraped it up: a sandwich baggie with a fold of bills weighted with a handful of change. "The crush-proof box if they got it, Sugar, don't forget," she yelled down. "Thank you!"

Mickey dragged me down the street to the Shell convenience store instead so that he could get some snacks. He whistled as he raced around the aisles, grabbing an armload of Gatorades and gummy bears and Tootsie Roll Pops. At the counter, Mickey rattled off Charlotte's brand—"Benson and Hedges Deluxe Ultra-Light Menthol 100s in a crush-proof box"—and then he asked for a pouch of Drum with a pack of papers. He peeled off a few of the bills from the wad in her baggie, ripped apart his camouflage nylon Velcro wallet, and stashed the change.

I asked for a single pack of Camel Lights. I got carded.

"Do I really not even look *eighteen*? I mean, come on."

Mickey gave me a sympathetic, one-sided grin. "I come in here at least two or three times a day," he said.

I never in a million years would have imagined it was a single girl barely old enough to drink who lived in Charlotte's apartment. The rents on all the Stein Properties were legendary. I'd seen the evidence myself, just a few months before, when I was trying to chase down a place to live with Hutch for the summer. Whenever you saw a house or an apartment for lease in Clarke County with high ceilings, honeyed hardwood floors, glossy white fireplace mantels, crown moldings, pristine subway tiles, and screened porches...Stein Properties. And you would not be surprised that you couldn't afford it. I'd found and mourned a handful of them.

An engraved stone tile above the entrance to her building read "1925." The door was propped open with a brick.

Charlotte met us at the top of the stairs in way too much makeup and a champagne-colored slip, like she thought she was Maggie the Cat. She wore those little kitten-heeled slippers with the poof at the toe and an overlong strand of pearls. She was impossibly tiny to be so voluptuous and have such pronounced facial features. Her eyes were drawn beyond their bounds and weighted down with false lashes. Her mouth was enormous, a beaming smile of horsey teeth framed by red-stained lips.

"Ah, thank you, Sugar!" She took the carton of cigarettes from Mickey the way a pageant queen accepts a bouquet of long-stemmed roses. She cradled the box in one arm and hugged him around the neck with the other. Her eyes closed as she savored the embrace, and she made a humming sound of barely contained pleasure when he kissed her wetly on the mouth. She playfully shoved him over the threshold and turned back to me.

Her lipstick was smeared, a little patch of it on her front teeth. It occurred to me that she might have put on her makeup while drunk. She took me by the wrist and leaned back as if about to dance with me. "Sugar, you must be Russell." She looked me up and down, appraising, admiring, and shaking her head slowly back and forth as if the sight of me in my white polo shirt and seersucker shorts with docksides was too much for words. "I'm Charlotte. Charlotte O'Brien. I have heard just tons of wonderful things about you, Sugar. Get in here, right this minute."

"Please, call me Rusty," I said.

"Of course!" she purred, cutting her eyes up in a mock show of having only just at that moment discovered my orange hair. She actually stretched up on tiptoe and *tousled* it. I thought tousling happened only in novels and movies, something people did to establish a familial bond between adults and children. But there was no other word for the gesture.

"Come in, come in." She breezed around the back of an armchair and motioned toward a pair of white, linen-covered love seats. "Sit, please. Make yourself comfortable."

The apartment resembled a beach cottage in a magazine. All the fabrics were impractically white or a nearly colorless pastel close to it. The antique French furniture was either white-washed, distressed, or pickled, heirlooms sandblasted by a hurricane of coastal affluence and shabby cast-off taste. No doubt an eclectic mix of the Princess bedroom set she'd had as a kid, filled out with all the old wicker from when her mama last had the cabana redone.

In case you saw the room before she'd had a chance to remind you that she came from low-country money, shells artfully littered every available surface along with jars of sea glass. They were accented by a framed portrait of her family on St. Simons Island, posed in front of a park of broad old oaks dripping with Spanish moss. In the distance sat a white mansion fronted by columns and black metal railings in the shape of wrought-iron vines.

If I hadn't already heard the rumors that the house in the photo was really her home, I would have thought the scene straight out of an Olan Mills portrait backdrop. It reminded me of my fifth-grade school picture, where I'm wearing a pearl-snap cowboy plaid shirt and leaning against an old wagon wheel in front of a too-flat backdrop of a split-rail fence.

I moved toward the sofa facing the French doors that led out onto the porch. An ancient lavender-point Siamese cat glared at me and abandoned her spot for a deep windowsill.

"Sugar, that's old Bridget. She's been with me since I was a girl. Tried to leave her at home when I first came to school. Mama called me every day for a week and made me listen to that poor thing squalling over the phone. I couldn't bear it. Had to run down and fetch her."

Charlotte smiled when she talked in a way that made me anticipate a punch line that never came. I just uncomfortably—stupidly—grinned back.

She dropped onto the matching sofa directly across from me, crossed her legs, began bouncing a dangling slipper from the end of one foot—yes, honest to God, she did that—and let out an extravagant sigh. "Can I offer you something cool to drink?" She looked at me sideways in a way that suggested a great conspiracy. "I made the most delicious-looking pitcher of whiskey lemonade, if I'm allowed to say so myself. Fresh-squeezed, with just a touch more Jim Beam than Nana's recipe ever called for." She chuckled and bit her pearls. "I know it's not even noon, but..."

I flashed her my movie star smile, the one I used to great success when I met my friends' mothers, and raised my hands in good-natured surrender. "It *is* July."

"Reason enough, Sugar. Reason enough!"

Mickey was in the kitchen behind an open refrigerator door making room for his Gatorades. She called out to him. "Sugar, will you bring that beautiful crystal pitcher of lemonade in here?"

"Which glasses do you want to use?" he yelled back.

"The tall heavy tumblers in the drainer by the sink. You know the ones I like to use for iced tea. Oh! And there's a dish of crushed ice in the freezer with some sprigs of fresh mint from the window box. Put it all on a nice serving tray for us, won't you, Sugar?" She winked at me.

Mickey came to the door and pointed at me. "You want one of these Gatorades? Or some sweet tea?"

"Iced tea would be great. Water's fine," I said.

"Nonsense, Sugar," Charlotte said to Mickey. "He's got to try my whiskey lemonade."

I raised my eyebrows at Mickey, hoping he'd know the best thing to say to rescue me without offending her.

"Honey, Rusty doesn't drink alcohol," he said in the lightly patronizing voice you'd use to deny a child.

"What?" She turned to me as if she couldn't believe it.

"I'm sure the lemonade is delicious," I winced. "But, yeah, I can't drink."

"Recovering?" she asked me with a lowered voice and sincere expression.

"No, I actually partake of just about anything and everything else. Alcohol just doesn't...agree with me."

"It makes him mean as hell," Mickey yelled from the kitchen. "He gets thrown out of bars and shit. I've seen it."

I spread my hands in silent admission.

Charlotte looked me up and down. "I can't even imagine you doing such a thing."

I gave her an apologetic lopsided grin.

"Well, at least join me for a cigarette then." She arched and leaned back, stretching the carton of cigarettes toward Mickey. "Sugar, before you finish up with the drink tray, will you come open this box, get me out a fresh pack, and then put the rest in the freezer?"

Mickey was immediately at her side to take it from her, with a strange little formal bow. "I most certainly will." I could have sworn he clicked his heels together.

"Oh, and Sugar, line up those packs nice and neat for me in the little rack, will you please? All the labels facing out in the same direction."

"Most certainly," he said. "I'd be happy to."

"Ah, thank you, Sugar." She brought her smile around and leaned toward me across the coffee table. In a stage whisper she confided, "He's just precious, isn't he?"

I shrugged, at a loss for how to add to a compliment that rich. "Mickey's a good guy. The first friend I made in Athens, actually."

Her mouth dropped open, as if in a shock of joyful surprise. "Is that right?"

"Yeah, we met last summer, at Freshman Orientation."

I smiled, watching Mickey slow walk from the kitchen with a laden silver tray. He sure had gone townie fast. Just a year ago, he was this talkative, clean-cut stoner from Savannah in R.E.M. T-shirts, acid-washed jeans, and high-top Converse All Stars. When I saw him again at the start of school a month later, he'd already fallen into that huge clothes pile at the Value Village thrift store and come out in full Athens anti-fashion. Now here he was serving sweet tea and whiskey lemonade wearing long-john bottoms under frayed, ill-sized, cut-off blue jean shorts, held in a wad at his waist with a big brown belt that probably once belonged to somebody's dead blue-collar uncle. An ironic T-shirt advertising a vacation Bible school peeked from underneath an old-man pajama top. He had tube socks and Doc Martens on one end and a black *Clockwork Orange* bowler hat on the other. Nobody else did the hat; that was Mickey's signature touch.

Because of the work clothes I had to wear—some of which I bought with an employee discount, others I shoplifted inside the requisite blazer by casually draping them over my arm on the way out of the store at the end of my shift—it was easiest for me to set myself apart by moving through townie culture in the glaring foundational garments of legitimate prep school uniforms, elaborated to the point of costume. I wore cuffed high-water khakis, pastel button-down shirts, the fat knit ties we'd worn since junior high, docksides, penny loafers, saddle oxfords, and vintage oxblood wingtips. No socks. Never socks. Maybe an overstated argyle in the dead of winter. But there were rules—old rules—no chancy creativity required.

There were hundreds of places I could totally

blend, with the exception being nearly everywhere I most wanted to go—from leather bars in Atlanta to the progressive music venues that Athens was famous for: the Georgia Theater, Uptown Lounge, Rockfish Palace, and The 40 Watt Club.

I knew I couldn't pull off actual cool—original cool—so I tried to pass off what I had as "intentionally ironic." In the crush of redneck punk, Southern Goth, and deconstructed farmer flannel, I did vintage prep.

"I wasn't remotely interested in SEC football or rushing frats," I told Charlotte. "And neither was Mickey. So we spent the free time we had between orientation lectures, campus tours, and placement exams going through the crates at Wuxtry Records and checking out the bands playing around town. We smoked a *lot* of pot." Mickey flashed me a Cheshire Cat grin. "We clicked."

Charlotte shook her head slowly from side to side, her eyes looking a bit misty. "Sugar, there's just something truly magical about the friendships you form when you go away to school, isn't there? Haven't you found that to be true?"

After carefully placing our drinks on coasters, Mickey served up the tiny blotter hits of acid with a pair of tweezers.

"Are those my good tweezers from the medicine cabinet?" Charlotte slapped at him. "I hope you wiped those off with a Kleenex before trying to stick them in our company's mouth!"

I took the little paper square on my fingertip first

and transferred it to my tongue, trying not to grimace too much. I hated that notebook paper taste. Charlotte pinched hers between the nails of her thumb and index finger, placed it in her mouth like a tiny hors d'oeuvre, and grinned like the devil. Mickey licked his off the tweezers and ground it between his front teeth, like the irritatingly small and flavorless remains of chewing gum.

A half-hour later, after a canned dialogue of antebellum pleasantries and loquacious flattering chitchat, the prevailing sense of the acid's metallic taste gave over to the discomfort of pre-trip sweats.

Starting to trip is much like the approach of a storm. First, there's the pacing, the foot-bouncing, the grinning, and the waiting—motion without movement. Then there's the anxious perspiration where excitement and anticipation become confused with worry and fear. At some point you discover that many of the same hormones released by those emotions have been handed over to the effects of the drug itself. It's like when you realize the sound of leaves rattling against one another in the wind has given way to the patter of rain drops, and as soon as you can process that subtle change, only seconds later there's the shocking roar of a downpour on the roof, and sheets of water blur the view through the windows. A trip starts as a similarly small, internal sensation and then turns inside out—until you find yourself within *it*, swallowed by it. Seeing, hearing, feeling it from the inside. At its most powerful, you can sit in the middle of the whirling wall, suspended in a center too still to be touched.

Electric, velvet-flocked white-on-white damask patterns had started to surface on the plain plaster walls when Charlotte cried out, "Oh! Nina Simone!" and flew across the room to turn up the volume on the stereo.

A voodooienne was singing about wanting some sugar in her bowl.

"Oh, how I adore her." She clasped her hands to her chest and then threw them out toward Mickey. "Sugar, come dance with me!"

Bridget and I shared a few uncomfortable minutes as fellow wallflowers while Charlotte and Mickey writhed and sort of faux-tangoed around the room. I kept waiting for some crack in her performance. The character she played was so unoriginal, it seemed like she should at least slip from time to time into the naturally more complex yet mundane reality of whoever she really was underneath that thin layer of smoke.

I hadn't moved from the first seat I'd landed in. I had, in fact, been rooted to the spot for hours. It never occurred to me to explore the apartment further or even go to the bathroom.

During a lull between records, I realized that I was straining to listen to a pair of voices. An argument, between a man and a woman. It sounded like it was coming from the porch. Even going back to my first time smoking pot at fifteen, my experimentation with drugs had always been at least partially motivated by a desire to enhance my perception of the supernatural.

I finally broke down and asked if there was somebody out there.

Charlotte's eyes glittered, slightly unfocused. She crawled closer, drifted up onto the love seat beside me, and nearly straddled my knee. With the acid kicked in, the most noteworthy change in her behavior seemed to be a diminished awareness of personal space. Or maybe it was only that my sensitivity to her domineering, sultry physicality had intensified.

"You hear them, don't you?" She suppressed a squeal.

Mickey's head popped up over my shoulder. He had been lying on the floor behind the sofa watching the ceiling fan rock and whir. "You can hear them?" He was excited too. "I told her, if anybody else could hear them, brother, it'd be you."

"Shh!" Charlotte hissed.

We all froze, eyes glazed in unison, listening.

"Who is that?" I asked. "Next-door neighbors? It sounds like they're on your porch."

Charlotte looked to Mickey, telepathically asking if she should tell me. He nodded.

"Spirits, Sugar. Ghosts."

"Hutch and I had a ghost this past year in our dorm room," I said, looking over to Mickey for corroboration. "We found out his name using a Ouija board."

I admit, I expected her to ask to hear *my* ghost story. But, without missing a beat, she deftly folded my line into her monologue. "I sure would love to know who mine are. I've been listening for their names for months and I still don't have the first clue. I can tell you they're an angry couple passionately caught somewhere between loving and hating each other. From what I've been able to gather, they were the first tenants who lived in this apartment, right after it was built. Well, actually, I don't know that they both lived here. I think she lived here and he just visited. Stayed the night every now and then, if you know what I mean. They were living in sin or having some torrid affair, either one. Isn't it just delicious to think of it? I love the twenties. I'm convinced that I must have lived then."

"Maybe this place is connected to a past life," I said.

"Oh, Sugar, yes! I have often thought the very same thing. I've sometimes wondered if I might not even *be* her. Or if I knew her, at least. I felt her presence when I was first shown the apartment. I had to live here. It felt like it was my home. And the thought of anybody else living in it made me raving mad. Speaking of raving, my daddy was fit to be tied when he found out how much the rent was, but I'd already signed the lease. There was nothing he could do about it."

The music ended. The record player arm lifted. The voices had also stopped.

I was still half convinced we would open that door and find a couple sitting out there on a break from their fight. I could see them in my mind's eye, smoking, sulking in separate corners, catching their breath.

I wanted badly to go out onto the porch. I needed to see that there was really no one there. I said as much to Charlotte.

"Oh, it's getting dark now. We should go out there anyway. Watch the sunset. Light some candles. Sugar, change the record over," she said to Mickey. She turned to me and confided, "I think the music draws them."

Charlotte went over to a column of drawers set into the wall beside the Murphy bed closet doors. "Now, my Nana McMahon had a spirit table in her front parlor, with the prettiest little glass planchette. When she died, my mama and her sisters fought over that thing. The way they acted, you would have thought she'd hollowed out the legs and stashed cash money up inside there." She produced a Parker Brothers Ouija board with no box and unfolded it before me with a sigh. "But we're gonna have to make do with this. Not exactly steeped in history, but it'll work, won't it?"

She fluttered about, lighting candles inside the apartment. She ordered me to take care of a few hurricane lanterns and a scattering of votive candles out on the porch.

The French doors that led outside were like a portal to another dimension, a gateway to another time— the twilight with the street lamps—except for the cars swishing by trailing stereo fragments. The great magnolias just outside made the porch feel more hidden from view than I knew it really was. I felt like if I stayed out there too long I might not be able to get back.

Hearing raised voices again, I looked back through the golden rectangle of the door, all the way through the apartment into the kitchen. Mickey's bowler hat and Charlotte's Louise Brooks bob made me think for a moment that the spirits had somehow slipped around me and escaped inside to continue their argument. All night long Mickey had been begging her in low tones to let him play some of his music—probably Tones on Tail or Love and Rockets. I wondered what it was he had against Peter Murphy. She kept putting him off until "later."

Now it *was* later.

"No, Sugar! That's just not good séance music. When I said to change the record over, I meant flip this record over and play *the other side*."

I could think of several musical selections I'd prefer to explore myself, but when I was tripping that hard, I would have just as soon been alone in my room, lost in headphones. Within the context of the current scene, however, I too enjoyed the strict temporal immersion— the sense of time travel—that Billie Holliday and Nina Simone evoked. Even *The Color Purple* soundtrack passed the test of the intended vibe.

Charlotte joined me on the porch. She draped a printed silk scarf across the wicker and glass patio table to protect the Ouija board from the hard puddles of past candle drippings, pollen, and dust from the street. She had changed her necklace to a strand of jet beads with a tassel at the end, so long it swung down between her legs. "Nana's," she said, clutching the beads when I complimented them. "And this," she held out a black velvet smoking jacket with silk lapels, "belonged to my papa." She insisted I wear it while we reached into the past. She also brought along a battered antique leather scrapbook that she'd adapted into a journal, scratching notes on the heavy textured pages with a Montblanc fountain pen inset with mother-of-pearl.

Our session on the board was as tedious and cryptic as anybody would expect. Even though I'd witnessed compelling evidence in these types of situations before, I generally found divination tools to be a bit frustrating, even in the best of circumstances. Mickey puttered around in the background, ultimately producing a sandwich bag of weed and rolling a joint, which did little for our ability to read or spell. Charlotte was more obvious than most in her attempts to influence the planchette. She was writing a compelling fiction in which the female ghost in residence was "attached" to her and wanted to "speak through" her. The Ouija became the slowest form of typewriter she could have possibly chosen to author that story.

My fingertips hovered without resistance to her intentions. I reacted to the developments in her tale with barely feigned fascination. Hell, I would have been happy to dispense with the board altogether and willingly listen to the history she claimed to be channeling.

It essentially took us from 9:30 p.m. to 3:00 a.m. to produce the opening paragraph of an awkwardly composed and unedited gothic novel about a young woman named Clarissa whose lover abused her in that very apartment in 1926.

There was one distinctly riveting section—just a single line, but it must have taken half an hour to scrape it off the board. The spirit said something about making men want to hit her.

"Say that last part again." I squinted at Charlotte's handwriting on the journal page, upside down and illegible in all caps.

She read it back, enunciated but hushed, "I'm afraid there is something about me that drives men to physically hurt me."

"Whoa." I looked her straight in the eyes. "That's quite a confession."

She hugged her elbows, shuddered, and shook it away, a blunt edge of hair swinging along her jaw. "Heartbreaking," she said.

I suggested she try automatic writing, specifically that she try it *later*, on her own, after I'd gone. I assured her that I was eager to read the results of the story she would produce in my absence.

Around 2:00 a.m., Mickey crawled through a tear in the top corner of the screen, close to the crease where the porch overhang met the main roof of the building. He shimmied up a gutter and disappeared.

I watched him leave without acknowledgment. Charlotte had been deep in a series of revelatory one-word answers to leading questions. The digital 4:00

glowing in the living room broke the spell we were under. I realized he had been gone for two hours. "Where the hell did he go?"

Charlotte waved a dismissive hand and chuckled. "Sugar, he comes and goes like a stray cat."

She dragged me back inside, into the kitchen, where she tied on a ruffled apron and bustled about preparing a country breakfast. I tuned out much of the monologue that accompanied her cooking show performance, a rolling collection of boastful anecdotes about grandmothers and aunts and mouth-dripping memories of meals rendered in pornographic detail.

The front door buzzer sounded. Charlotte groaned, dashed down the stairs, and reappeared with Mickey.

"Someone moved the brick out of the door," he said, tucking a linen napkin into his collar.

The sleepless night and the bellies full of fatty food caught up with us. Everybody became quiet. Even Charlotte just smoked and smiled through slitlike eyes she could barely keep open. She insisted I stay and nap a little while before even thinking about driving anywhere. Mickey pulled down the Murphy bed and they collapsed into a white down duvet. I took off the velvet smoking jacket and smoothed it over the rounded arm of the sofa. At long last, Bridget returned to purr and make biscuits of her own against my side.

I got up to use the bathroom at some point and saw Mickey out on the porch, climbing through the rent in the screen and disappearing onto the roof again.

I was startled awake at noon. Charlotte was stalking around the kitchen, barefoot in a man's white dress shirt with the sleeves rolled up, and talking on a phone whose cord stretched away from the wall. She wasn't saying much, but I could hear the angry garble of a man's voice filling her ear. "Yes, Daddy...I heard you...I said I *heard* you. I don't want to talk about this anymore right now."

She slung a crash of silverware into the sink, and when she turned to slam the phone into its cradle, she saw me sitting up watching her.

"Oh, Sugar, I'm sorry to wake you like that." She flashed me her beaming smile, but not before I caught sight of a dark expression I had not yet seen on her features— the exact opposite of the sleepy-eyed bliss she usually presented—held breath and barely contained fury.

I lied and said I was already awake. "No need to apologize."

"Let's go back out onto the screened porch," she said. "After that conversation, I think I'll need to smoke two or three in a row."

While Charlotte pounded the cushions on her wicker divan, I sat watching the traffic down in the street, trying to wake up fully.

When she finally sat down—apropos of nothing, completely out of the blue—she said "I'm a witch, you know."

She had an unnerving way of speaking like she might be trying to seduce me. No matter the context or my sexual orientation or the fact that she was sleeping with one of my friends. Everything she said felt like it was intended to be a proposition of some kind.

"Is that right?" I couldn't help but smile at her. She demanded it somehow. Just pulled it right out of me. Maybe she *was* a witch.

"I thought Mickey might have mentioned it." She looked down at her lap and plucked at the hem of her shirt and then glanced up through her bangs, coy. "Or you might have heard a rumor."

She clearly wanted me to ask. She wanted me to be so curious that I couldn't withstand the impulse to beg for details about her magical powers.

"I did not know that about you," I said.

But just as if I'd read the next question in her script, she said, "I influence the weather."

I had intended to maintain a neutral facial expression, which I calculated would best thwart her dramatic lead. But the significance of that statement broke through.

"Why that face?" she asked. "I saw a flicker of something. Not at all what I expected." Her eyes narrowed. "And what I said was not at all what *you* expected. I've shocked you. But in an unpredictable way."

"I have to admit," I said, "it's...uncanny, really. One of my aunts was supposedly a witch. It was rumored that she could make it rain. *Widely believed* that she could make it rain, now that I think about it."

It was Charlotte's turn to ask, "Is that right?"

"Yep. That's specifically what she was known for: influencing the weather." I took a drag off my cigarette while maintaining sideways eye contact. I half-expected her to confess to some trick of knowing this obscure fact about my family. I couldn't think of anyone I might have told who could have shared that with her. I didn't really talk about many things that happened in my life before I moved to Athens. I didn't even think about most of them. "Not influencing. *Manipulating* the weather. I believe that's the expression we always heard."

Charlotte looked at her cigarette, not at me. "Did you see her do it?"

"I was never around that part of my family very much. My cousin Vicky, her youngest daughter, who's close in age to me, claimed to have inherited that know-how, that...talent. Or would you call it an ability?"

She pretended to consider, then shrugged and grinned. "All of the above."

"I did get to know Vicky a little bit better after Aunt Betsy died. I spent a week with her the summer before my junior year in high school."

"Just a few years ago, then. And did something happen?"

I looked off through the screen, seeking the details of the memory in the magnolia branches. "There was this one storm, this one time it rained really hard that... made me wonder. The timing seemed beyond coincidence."

I realized I was slowly nodding my head and that Charlotte was mimicking me. She looked smug. "I knew you'd believe me," she said.

I exhaled in a wordless sound of protest, a kind of laugh, a scoff. "I didn't say I believed you."

"Sugar, I can *tell*." She settled back into the cushions with a self-satisfied wiggle. "I know you know it's true."

I wanted to comment on the distinction between believing in something *generally* and believing *her*. But I wasn't really fully decided, so I kept the question to myself.

"So, y'all never tried cloudbusting when you were kids?" Charlotte asked.

"Cloudbusting? You mean like the Kate Bush song?"

"Love her," she gushed.

"Really?" I was genuinely surprised.

To prove it, she sat up straight and sang a few lines... of the wrong song. As I suspected, the only Kate Bush she knew was "Running Up That Hill," a melody that anyone with a radio had heard a million times. Even still, the lyrics were hardly close, and her vocal impersonation was embarrassing.

To hide my mortification, I said, "I didn't think you listened to any progressive music."

"I just don't care for *Mickey's* progressive stuff. That Tones on Tail he's obsessed with?" She rolled her eyes, gagged, and lit a new cigarette off the old one. "Irritates the hell out of me. It's so repetitive."

I silently conceded agreement with her on that.

"Anyway," she drew her legs up under the tail of her shirt and wrapped her arms around her knees, "the way we always did it—super simple—you lie on your back and look up at the sky. You pick out a white puffy cloud and then you try to use your mind to tear it into pieces. You can pick different clouds and race to see who can bust theirs up first. Or you can pick the same cloud, have everybody concentrate on it, and watch how it dissolves even faster." She paused to take a drag, looking satisfied with herself. "Sugar, I always won at that game. Busting them up was way too easy. So to challenge myself, I started trying to push different clouds into one another. Force them to join." She leaned toward me, her chin in her hand on a crossed knee, excited and conspiratorial. "Or move entire fronts toward each other until the friction produced a lightning storm."

I raised my eyebrows to let her know I was listening and capable of being significantly impressed at the right points in a story.

"It feels like when you try to touch the same ends of two magnets together," she continued. "And you want to know what the real secret is?" She didn't actually expect me to say anything. "Anger. Not just any old display of temper but the kind of frustration that boils up slowly, subsides a little, but lingers. Jealousy. Resentment. *Humiliation.*"

"Makes a kind of sense," I said. "The metaphors. Emotions and weather."

Her mood shifted back toward light and breezy, like a sunbeam breaking through a fast-moving overcast sky. "Sometimes I release a storm just for fun. Just to mess with people. You know, just to be wicked. I love to blow down some sorority girl hair. I'll wait for those boys in their blazers with their bed heads and their beer buzzes to come stumbling out of their cars down there by the Bottle Shop and leave those girls behind primping in the parking lot. I listen to them squealing in the wind, trying to roll the windows up as fast as they can. It amuses me. Dropping my storms all over those little parties I'm no longer welcome to attend, watching their hairspray run to glue in a matter of seconds, melting like cotton candy licked with lots of spit." For a moment, her face distorted like she might demonstrate. Then she managed to swallow and continue. "The Greeks come out on those big old antebellum porches, up and down Milledge, taking pictures—a bunch of colored-up, satin-wrapped, blow-dried Barbies. Lord, Sugar, haven't you heard the good news? Those girls have found a way to have homecoming and prom every other goddamned weekend of the fall. So I drop a little something on them every now and then. You've seen the evidence. All those grand old oaks up and down the Avenue. Been there for 100, 150 years. Now fallen, sawed flat into tree-stump coffee tables."

"Ah," I said. "I had no idea that was all your doing."

She went silent and looked away for a breath, her eyes unfocused. Then she seemed to realize something that she had not before. She continued in that earlier tone, bragging, bossy, instructive. "It's no surprise that tears and rain go together. Eventually, something will trigger a flash of thunder and lightning and you slip up. It all escapes from you. Slips out. The timing can be very inappropriate if you can't acknowledge that you're the one doing it. You can control it if you put your mind to it." Here she clenched her eyes shut and her left hand into a fist. "You have to think really hard—you have to feel really intensely—the kind of emotional pain that makes you mad. And then you point it where you want it to go. Like you're trying to blow out a candle from across the room...you let it go." She exhaled into a smile, uncurling her fist and releasing a tiny invisible dove off the palm of her hand.

"So," I said. "It's like making yourself cry."

She frowned, inhaled another deep drag, and blew it out of her pursed lips in a stream, just like a cartoon of a cloud on a windy day. "No. It's more like the opposite of crying. I don't cry."

"Me neither," I said. "I scream. But I hardly ever cry."

She continued silently smoking and watching me. I found myself nodding my head again, without making eye contact, twisting my lips in consideration. Skeptical, but entertaining all that she'd just told me.

Eventually she whispered, "I'm doing it right now. I've been doing it the whole time we've been out here."

"Who—or what—are you hating that much right now?" I asked. It was the first legitimate question that came to my mind.

"Oh, I'm hating my daddy." There it was again, that cruel flash I'd seen behind her beaming mask. The one I wasn't originally supposed to see. But now that she knew that I knew it was there, she exposed it to me without hesitation or apology. "What are you thinking about, Sugar?"

I was thinking about how much her voice had changed. That even though she still called me Sugar, the intensity of her put-on drawl had softened. When she spoke of these things—these magical, manipulative abilities she claimed to have—she seemed to become entirely serious, sober, and a lot less Scarlett.

Of course, I didn't feel like I could tell her that. But there was another layer of thought I could genuinely share without missing a beat. "I was thinking of all the songs about weather that I could put on a mixed tape. 'Rain' by The Cult. That Fleetwood Mac song 'Storms.'"

She cocked her head and frowned. "I don't think I've ever heard that one."

"No? God, it's one of Stevie Nicks' classics. Lesser known, for sure. It's on *Tusk*."

"What about 'Purple Rain?' " she asked. "Oh! And 'Here Comes the Rain Again.' "

"Prince? Hmm. Maybe," I said. "The Eurhythmics? Sure, I mean, that's pretty mainstream too, but you could build the whole playlist around 'Here Comes the Rain Again.' It could be the crescendo moment, the familiar pay-off track that everybody responds to, the one that just seems to crash across a room—"

She shushed me with a wordless gasp and turned her face toward the ceiling, to the sky beyond it. There was an opening scatter, like a handful of gravel hurled at a lover's window, and then the maraca rattle of the drops on the magnolia leaves.

Interrupted, my mouth remained hanging open. My eyes must have noticeably widened in shock at the sudden roar of the downpour because she pointed at my face and let out a single accusing burst of laughter.

"Right on cue," she said. "Beyond coincidence."

It took me a second to realize that the sound of applause was the rain.

TWO

A week passed, and I didn't see or hear from Mickey. I tried to get in touch with him going into the weekend—hanging out with him was my only hope of distracting myself from sitting around thinking about Hutch—but he never returned my calls. When I went by the Commune, a shirtless, barefoot hippy guy in board shorts—his name might have been TJ or CJ—told me through the screen door that Mickey hadn't been home. They assumed he was at Charlotte's.

"You know, his *girl*friend's!" somebody yelled from inside.

Ah. They thought I was pursuing Mickey. Like sexually, romantically. Of course I was offended, mostly that anybody would think Mickey, of all people, represented the relationship bar I had set for myself. It hurt my ambition more than my feelings. I'm sure I blushed, the curse of my coloring that makes me furious and results in only more blushing.

Why do straight guys assume we would want them when they are clearly not worth having? It takes so much more than a willing dick.

The gurgle of a bong was punctuated by coughed laughter. TJ/CJ looked over his shoulder into the house at whoever it was, giggled nervously, and then turned back to me. He visibly tried to compose himself. "Sorry, dude." As I turned to leave, he suddenly remembered something. "Oh, hey! If you do see him, though, tell him his dad's been calling here."

I drove back down South Lumpkin to the Five Points intersection at Milledge. While I waited for the light to change, I rolled down my window and looked up at Charlotte's apartment. There were a few dim lights on. It looked like the French doors leading in from the porch were ajar. The shadow of a ceiling fan flashed in the gap. There was no other sign of movement, no sounds of music.

It was all the way to Thursday of the second week— eleven days later—when Charlotte finally called. For once, I was actually hanging out at the apartment watching TV with my roommate Oliver and his girlfriend Staci.

When Oliver answered and looked over at me, I couldn't help but hope for a second it was going to be Hutch. But Oliver knew Hutch as well as he knew me. And Hutch was always on friendlier terms with everyone we mutually knew. Whoever it was, Oliver gave no happy sign of recognition.

"It's some old Southern lady," he whispered with his hand over the mouthpiece, passing me the phone. "It's not your mom."

"Sugar?"

"Hey, Charlotte. What's going on?"

"Oh, Sugar, I'm so sorry. Mickey has been asking me to call you but he couldn't remember your number. I finally dug around through a million-and-a-half scraps of paper in the bottom of his little satchel. Called three wrong numbers before this one—" She broke off with what sounded like a gasp for breath. When she tried to speak again, she swallowed her own voice. It sounded thick, like she was crying.

"What's wrong?" I asked.

"Oh, Sugar! It was awful. He fell!"

"Mickey *fell*? What are you talking about?"

"Sugar, he fell off the goddamned roof! Just like I knew he would. I kept telling him to use the stairs like a normal human being—"

"What! From the third floor? Is he in the hospital?"

"No, no, he's here. He was down at the other end of the building, where the jewelry store is, on the backside where it slopes down. It's really only one floor up from back there."

"Are you kidding me? Is he badly hurt?"

"Well, miracles never cease. Didn't break anything. A hedge took most of the momentum. He's scratched up more than anything. But he was upside down. And close enough to the ground to bang the top of his head really bad. Concussion, of course. Compressed his neck, but it's just kind of technically bruised or something. It's a wonder he's not dead or paralyzed."

"Did you call an ambulance?"

"No, Sugar, I was sitting here having a glass of merlot and wondering where the hell he was, and he came stumbling in with twigs in his hair and scrapes all over his face. He was white as a sheet. Not making a whole lot of sense, but enough that I gathered he'd fallen off the roof. Well, of course I insisted on driving him straight to the hospital."

"My God. Do his parents know? I went by the Commune and TJ or CJ or whatever his name is said that Mickey's dad has been calling trying to find him."

"They've spoken a few times. He's fine where he is."

When I asked if I could speak to Mickey, she ignored me and wrapped up the conversation. She said she just wanted me to know why I hadn't heard from them. She made sure I took down her number, Sugared me a few more times, and hung up.

THREE

I ended up one night in my car during a downpour, trying to have sex with a guy whose name I didn't even know. Truthfully, that's not as unusual as it may sound, nor is it normally worth reporting. Except for the fact that this time, I got busted for it.

Another week had gone by with no word from Mickey or Charlotte. No calls or letters or postcards from Hutch, either. Summer break was pretty much over. Rush week was happening; people were moving back into the dorms.

I was finally getting to move out of my temporary summer living situation. It took me only a couple of sporadic afternoon packing sessions to box up my meager collection of things. I was waiting for my new roommates to get back into town—a couple of girlfriends this time. We had leased a cottage next door to the Commune, of all places. We didn't intentionally choose it because of that particular proximity; it just kind of worked out that way: 1989 South Lumpkin Street, just past Hope.

Time and place were coming together in an undeniably cosmic synchronicity. I could only imagine what it was going to be like trying to study or sleep next door to that much round-the-clock extracurricular activity. Or find a parking space, for that matter.

In anticipation of the move, I dropped by the new cottage early that evening, mostly just to peek in the windows. There was a truck in the drive, drop cloths and paint cans on the floor. They were obviously still working to get it ready for us. The landlord had told me that I couldn't pick up the keys until the day before the lease started, but I could daydream about what it was going to be like living there. It was a small place for three people, but it had a lot more character than any apartment complex.

When I walked back toward the street where I'd left my car, I saw this cute, curly-haired blond guy leaving the Commune—real preppy-looking, frat-boy type probably there to pick up drugs. The sun had gone down, low storm clouds hastening the gloom, but I could still tell that he was staring at me, more openly than I would have expected. With virtually no facial expression, he said, "Hey."

He had obviously parked his car close to mine. As I dug my keys out of my pocket, he lifted his chin toward my car and asked, "What year is that?" with the same bored inflection.

"Seventy-nine. Mercedes-Benz 280SE," I said, matching his nonchalance, at least in tone.

"Cool." He was driving an orangey-red two-door BMW 325i, probably four or five years old. He waited for me to pull out first, drumming on his steering wheel and singing loudly to U2's "Where the Streets Have No Name," and then he followed me down West Lake. He pulled up beside me at an intersection. Now I could hear "I Still Haven't Found What I'm Looking For." He mouthed the words at me, completely cheesy, totally risking any sex appeal he might have, if he was indeed cruising me. He tailed me all the way back to College Center Apartments. He pulled up beside me, rolled down his passenger window, and turned down "With or Without You" before I could even get out.

I rolled down my window too.

"So, do you have a place?" he asked.

For a moment, his cocky entitlement produced a sadistic need in me to play it straight, just to see what his deflation would look like. But after a freshmen year spent in disappointment at all the guys who were still in the closet, his boldness worked for me. I found it refreshing.

"I'm actually in the process of moving out of here," I said. "I have roommates, anyway."

"Aw, man, that sucks." He looked straight ahead through the windshield. I could tell he was struggling to think of something to say.

"What about you?" I asked.

He winced an apology. "Theta Chi house. Rush week."

"Ah. Is it now?" I felt he should know that there were places in the universe where Greek life went entirely unnoticed. And that there were people for whom his affiliations held no currency.

"Know anywhere else we could go?" He had the fullest lower lip I'd ever seen on a white guy.

"I have an idea," I said.

"Is it cool if I leave my car here and we take yours?"

"Sure."

He was visibly perspiring, with wet puppet-mouth shapes under his arms and a perfect, dewy line above his top lip. As he buckled his seatbelt, I watched a single large drop of sweat trace a snail track from his temple to his jaw, hang there for a second, and then dive onto the surface of his collar. He smelled faintly like clean hay and the Mennen Speed Stick deodorant that every boy in junior high layered beneath his Polo cologne. His hair reminded me of Michelangelo's *David.* His clothes were confusing—terrible, really—a white golf shirt, tight white jeans with a slash of blue ballpoint ink on the knee, and white leather Tretorn tennis shoes with ankle socks. Maybe it was a uniform, like he worked at a country club or something. I certainly hoped so.

I had been listening to Morrissey's solo album *Viva Hate* on the way to College Center. Ironically, this was not the time to share the gayest end of my musical taste. I wasn't thinking about the stereo being on, and when I cranked the engine we were blasted by the mortifyingly fay chorus of "Hairdresser on Fire." I punched the eject button and tossed the cassette over my shoulder into the backseat, like a grenade.

He sort of chuckled scornfully and muttered, "Morrissey."

I glanced over to find him smirking. "You recognized it," I said. But I still felt my face burning. I grabbed a tape with the first two R.E.M. albums and popped in the *Reckoning* side.

We engaged in that most petty of small talk that men make when hooking up. It's different from the dialogue in the first few minutes of a porn film, but it's probably still just as awkward, and definitely just as pointless. The part of me that observed these scenes from outside my body couldn't seem to help but fixate on the voices we adopted: self-consciously masculine and deeper than what was comfortably sustainable. Whatever that collective impulse was—some ideal opposite of the effeminacy we feared more than anything—it had this way of homogenizing our speech, regardless of where we hailed from, into something like "surfers" in an episode of *Afterschool Special.*

We literally talked about the weather.

"It's about to come down, man." He'd dropped into the lowest part of his baritone that he could manage. Quieter. Maybe he'd reached that point in the anticipation that qualifies as turned on. Or maybe, contrary to all his brash initiative, he was genuinely nervous.

"Yep," I said—so banal—squinting through the

windshield at the sky. It was darker than usual for so early in the evening, tinted the ghoulish green we associate with tornado weather in the South. "Here it comes."

Right on cue, the saloon-flavored nostalgia of "So. Central Rain" jangled from the speakers.

The drops that splattered the windshield were fat and far between. I turned onto Milledge Circle, the side street with the entrance into that back parking lot behind Charlotte's building. I pulled behind the Dumpster into the space-that-wasn't-a-space just seconds before the sky opened up. Walls of water fell around us.

I wouldn't necessarily kiss in a situation like that, but he seemed eager to, and after all, it was his lips that had sold me. His mouth tasted like Wrigley's Spearmint gum and chamomile. Before I closed my eyes, I noticed a curtain of rain sliding off a section of roof right in front of the car. The roof declined to a lower level behind one of the first-floor shops, creating a sort of back porch entryway. There were dangling screws and torn open collars of aluminum; a gutter was missing. The water fell like wet silver hair into a row of boxwood shrubs.

In a flash of lightning I could see where Mickey must have gone over the edge. I squeezed my eyes shut for a moment at the thought of it. I shuddered. White-jeans guy pulled my T-shirt over my head. With the ignition off and the struggling AC gone, the windows were fogging over fast.

He looked even more like the *David* when he peeled

off his clothes. Underneath those hideous white jeans he had impressive runner's legs. I felt inadequate for a moment, but then this was the part where comparison gave way to conquest. Being able to *have* him was at least *equal to* him. His skin was the same pale color as mine, only more perfectly uniform, without the freckles I have on my shoulders, chest, and forearms. I didn't have a problem acknowledging that my skin was probably one of my best features, especially among people our age. It was one of those things girls coveted and commented on.

Other men, not so much.

I constantly worried about being too "pretty" to appeal to guys. I'm technically a ginger, but with brownish-gold body hair, more like a hairy blond. Not like the bright copper-penny hair with the matching orange bush and the purple-tinted cock. Those poor guys are fucking *pariahs*. My chest hair was just starting to fill in, so I was biding my time. I figured by thirty I'd probably have a decent "ruddy lumberjack" thing going for me.

The rain roared on the roof on the car, punctuated by a smattering of crushed ice exactly the size of the pellets that come out of a convenience store soda machine. In a matter of seconds the hail was drowned and melted by a warmer torrent. The water came down so hard that all horizontal surfaces were hazed with ricocheted spray.

I could not have envisioned conditions in which it would have been less likely to be busted by a cop for having sex in a car.

But that's exactly what happened.

He had let down the passenger seat and laid back. I was in a plank position on top of him, so I saw the fractured blue lights melting in a kaleidoscope on the back window. Even though the patrol car was clearly blocking us in, it didn't occur to me that it was there for us. We heard the single staccato bloop of the siren, that "friendly" setting that sounds like an old arcade game.

We broke off kissing. Looking back, it was a blessing we hadn't gone any further. And when I saw the silhouette of a figure sliding along the car windows, already on top of us, I rolled back into the driver's seat, banging my hip on the emergency brake.

"Shit!" I scrabbled around on the floorboard for my shorts and yanked them up around my knees. He was having a much harder time with those wretched long, tight jeans, what with all the moisture in the air. I was aware of his bare hips and only partially deflated erection bucking up into plain view as a presence loomed at my driver's side window.

There was a knuckle rap on the glass and—most horrifying of all components that could have possibly been added to the scene—the beam of a flashlight illuminated our state of undress.

"Ohmygodohmygodohmygod." He was almost moaning as he tried to get the jeans up around his waist, zip them, and raise the seat to its normal upright position, all in one motion.

The officer knocked again. "Open up, please."

I rolled the window down, squinting into the pouring rain and the bright light. I shielded my eyes with my hand, which felt awkwardly like I was saluting the policeman in a sarcastic or defiant gesture. I hoped he wouldn't think that. The light swung past me to my shirtless companion. His skin glowed like a bioluminescent creature, the fish in a lake at the bottom of a cave: blue irises without pupils and disheveled Greek demigod hair backlit by fogged glass and gold streetlight.

The light fell back on me. "You gentlemen want to explain what you're doing back here?"

I huffed wordlessly and spread my hands apart in a gesture that asked, "What does it look like?"

The officer—"Brody," his brass nameplate read—officiously demanded to see my license and insurance. Surreally, almost like the script of a crime drama, he specifically said "insurance" and not "registration." Why do they always say "license and registration" in the movies? Is that a California thing? He asked to see my passenger's ID as well.

I dug my cards out of my wallet and handed it all through the window.

He checked the photos briefly against our faces, told us to sit tight, and walked back to the patrol car.

I rolled up the window and scraped the water from my eyebrows with my index fingers. "Oh, jeez," I muttered.

"This cannot be happening," he said, his voice high

and strained. "This would never happen in Atlanta. They'd just tell us to get a room and let us go."

"By the way, I'm Rusty Stewart," I said. "Since it might look even worse if we admit we haven't met yet."

"Gavin. Van Holland. We *cannot* get arrested for this." He sighed miserably and wiped a clear spot on his window with the heel of his hand. He alternated peering into the side mirror with twisting around in his seat to look over his shoulder. "What's taking so long? What's he doing?"

"Maybe he's waiting for the rain to stop."

It had slowed to a light drizzle. Most of the larger drops were falling from the wet upper branches of trees. Officer Brody came back and asked me if I had a problem showing him the contents of my trunk.

"No. That's fine." I was eager to be cooperative. "You can check it out."

He told Gavin to stay where he was and held the door open while I climbed out. There was nothing in the trunk except for the crates of records and CDs. It looked like some kind of contraband all gathered together that way. I felt guilty somehow.

"I'm in the process of moving," I explained. "I wanted to keep all my music with me overnight, where I could at least lock it up out of sight."

None of the shops along that street were music stores. Besides, surely he wouldn't think I would sell any of *this* vinyl. It was all valuable imports—alphabetized and sleeved in heavy plastic—not that cheap, shrink-wrapped shit for sale in stores. Every piece was meticulously labeled in my own handwriting, in case I needed to point that out as proof of how long I'd had them. Clearly, they hadn't been hastily acquired from anywhere.

Officer Brody insisted on taking the crates out and setting them on the wet asphalt. On impulse, I reached to help him. He waved me back; I hovered.

Once the trunk was empty, Brody lifted up the carpet flap and felt around the spare tire. He examined the bottom of a can of WD-40, felt the heft of its weight by tossing it lightly from hand to hand, and then he turned it away from the car and sprayed a piss stream of grease into the weeds. He must have thought it might be one of those decoy safes they sell in head shops, the ones that look like common household products on the outside, but with hollow cavities on the inside for hiding drugs. It made me nauseous that he suspected me of having one.

He knocked on the side of the car and called out, "Mr. Van Holland, can you come back here and join us, please?"

Gavin shuffled barefoot to the end of the Mercedes, managing to look pitiful and petulant at the same time.

Brody asked him, "Would you like to state for the record why you gentlemen are parked back here?"

Gavin's shirt was on inside out and bunched up at the back of the neck. "Um...parking. You know, *parking*." He spread his arms helplessly. "Fooling around."

Brody turned to me. "And Mr. Stewart, neither you nor Mr. Van Holland has a more appropriate place to have sex than in your car?"

"No. Not really."

"Neither one of you lives in these apartments?"

We both shook our heads.

"I have a friend who lives in 3A," I volunteered. *Why?* I just blurted it out. "Charlotte O'Brien. This is like...my space when I visit her." It was my honest reason for having picked this place.

Brody's gaze swung back and forth between us. "Are either of you aware that these shops have been repeatedly burglarized in the last month?" He emphasized his words with his hands.

We both shook our heads again, more vigorously this time, frowning with exaggerated facial expressions that we hoped made it clear we could not possibly have known such a thing.

"You are not here with the intentions of breaking and entering?"

"No, of course not!" I said. That came out more defensive and panicked than I would have liked. "I mean, it's pretty clear what we're doing, isn't it?"

Brody studied a small notebook in his hand. "Residents have reported seeing somebody on the roof." Then he peered back up at us through his eyebrows. "Know anything about that?"

"Nope." Now I really was lying. "If we were the robbers, wouldn't we run for it? Get away from here? I mean, come on—we wouldn't hang around on the roof or stop to fool around in a car, would we?" It came out of my mouth a bit strident and pissy.

"Not unless you're stupid," Brody muttered.

I was oddly comforted by his sudden layman's detour from the script.

We heard the rain starting up again, coming through the trees. Storms are sloppy rings. We must have been sitting under the calm eye and now the other side of the circle was about to arrive.

I begged Brody to let me put the record crates back in my trunk. "Sir, please. This collection is worth a lot of money."

He glanced up at the sky, sighed, and nodded, now looking a bit weary and miserable himself.

"Can I have that?" Brody indicated a small shop towel I kept in the trunk for drying off the car when I washed it or whatever else I might need it for.

"Yeah, sure. Take it." I hated myself for sounding so ingratiating.

While I loaded the trunk back up, as quickly as I could—by myself—Officer Brody walked Gavin around to the passenger side of my car and said something to him that I couldn't hear.

"I can't think of any reason why I should see you

here again," he said to me as he trotted by on the way back to his car. "Got it?"

"I understand. Absolutely. Thank you." My groveling was practically instinct.

I shut the trunk at the same moment he shut the patrol car door. The sound was loud. I realized I was shirtless, in the rain, in the glare of those damned rotating lights. I looked up at the windows of the apartments overlooking the back parking lot and saw the silhouettes of Charlotte's neighbors watching from several of them.

I telepathically pleaded with Officer Brody to turn off the light show. Behind his visor mirror he was mopping water off his crew cut with my towel and pressing the folded corners into his eye sockets.

"God, is he ever going to cut those lights?" Gavin whined, when I slid back into the driver's seat. He was fully dressed again, shirt right-side out.

"I know. Really." I turned my face toward him as I pressed my chest into the steering wheel, feeling around on the floorboard for my discarded shirt.

Brody followed us in the patrol car for several blocks back down South Lumpkin, until I pulled onto West Lake to head back to my old apartment. I could barely see. The windshield wipers were cranked on high and I had the AC defrost on full blast, slowly blowing a spreading hole in the fogged-up glass.

"Did that really just happen?" Gavin bounced up

and down in his seat. He was giddy, like we'd just seen an amazing show or a really good action movie. He proceeded to relive the entire experience, with the additional animated commentary of what he'd been thinking and feeling at each point in the scene. His voice was different; he spoke quickly and talked with his hands. He seemed much gayer now.

When we got back to College Center, I pulled into the space beside his BMW, cut the engine, sat back, and exhaled. I must have been holding my breath for the last hour.

Gavin made no move to get out of the car. He was watching me, turned toward me in his seat with his back leaned up against the door. He grinned.

"What?" I asked. "We are not doing anything else in this car."

He laughed. "No, I know. I was just wondering about something."

"What?"

"Whether or not you have a boyfriend."

Of course, thinking of Hutch, I could have complicated my answer. But after a pause that I hoped was short enough to go unnoticed, I went with the simple truth: "No," I said. "I don't."

"Then we should go out," he said. "Like, on a real date."

I shrugged. "Okay. Sure." I wasn't sure at all, in

fact, but I made a big show of finding a pen in the glove compartment and tearing two empty corners off an oil change invoice.

He wrote on his left knee, the one with the ink line. He printed his name in all caps, the digits without any dashes.

"This is my number for only a couple more days," I warned, handing him mine. "I don't know the new one by heart. It's not hooked up yet." I had, however, immediately sent a carefully cheerful, brief card to Hutch's parents' house in Tennessee with my new phone number. His mother always praised me for being thoughtful and responsible and *well mannered*. At some point he'd come home from New York, and she'd give it to him. I wondered what he'd say when she asked him why we weren't going to be "roommates" again this year.

Gavin opened his door but leaned in to kiss me before he jumped out. I let him. "I'll talk to you tomorrow." The surface of his eyes looked glossy wet.

FOUR

I had only a handful of shifts left at Macy's and even fewer nights in the apartment with the guys. When I got home from work the evening after I'd met Gavin, my roommate Oliver handed me a note, a smug expression on his face. I snatched it from him, thinking, *Finally, Hutch*, but just as quickly I realized there was no reason why Hutch's calling would put a shit-eating grin on Oliver's face. It was another scrap of paper with Gavin's name and number scrawled on it.

"Man, this guy has called for you, seriously, like ten times," Oliver said.

Cliff, the roommate I'd been sharing a bedroom with all summer, crossed his arms and gravely bobbed his head to corroborate the extreme statistics. "The last time he called, he made Ollie read his number back to him to prove that he'd actually written it down."

"No shit!" Oliver testified. "He didn't really sound that gay, though."

"Oh, fuck you," I said, with a weary sigh.

"Oliver!" Cliff said in a scolding, fatherly tone, but the pretend outrage dissolved into a fit of giggling.

"What?" Oliver asked, lifting his arms and spreading his hands in innocence, an impish smirk on his face.

After I'd stretched the phone cord into my room and shut the door for some privacy, they started whooping, wolf-whistling, and catcalling. Intellectually, I knew their attention was meant to communicate acceptance. They would have given me the same kind of shit if it had been a girl calling. Even still, their hazing felt an awful lot—too much—like real bullying. My body responded with involuntary shame, that violent flush that crept up my neck and into my cheeks. They didn't have to see it to bust me. I heard Oliver shout "Rosy!"—the name they'd taken to childishly calling me when they caught me blushing.

Gavin picked up at the end of the first full ring. The "Hello?" sounded a little deadpan. But when I asked to speak to him, and he realized it was me, I could hear a smile shift into his voice. "Hey. How are you?"

So began another awkward back-and-forth attempt at making small talk. He asked me if I'd been "keeping dry out there" and laughed at his own joke. Yes, we actually, literally, talked about the weather. Again. Other than that, we never talked about what happened that night.

This time, we exchanged the requisite information about majors. He was poli-sci, pre-law. Big shock there. I told him my mother had insisted that I start out pre-med.

Adventures of Bailey and Me

BRIANNA N. NAROZNY

ISBN:1495472221
ISBN-13:9781495472220

DEDICATION

This book is dedicated to my Mom, Dad,
Sister and Brother.

Also, to my best friends Ishika, Sloan, and Maayan
and all of the poorly treated and abused animals in the world.

CONTENTS

Acknowledgments   i

1   Getting Started…   8

2   Japan   11

3   Saving the World's Gentle Giants   13

4   Finding Help   16

5   Greece   18

6   India   21

7   Switzerland   23

8   Home on the Farm   27

ACKNOWLEDGMENTS

I would like to thank my friend's dog, Bailey, a character is this story.
has helped me to send the message that animals matter and have feelin
too.

*"Saving one animal won't change the world, but it will change t
world to that animal"* **Author Unknown**

...1 going to tell you a story about how I got where I am. There are some ...and downs to this story. So, let's get started.

...my name is Brooklyn but my friends and family call me Brook. I come ...n the United States of America but I travel around the world helping ...nals with my dog Bailey. So, here are some things about me: my parents ...me when I was 6 years old and I went to live in an orphanage. The ...hanage lets kids leave when they are at least 11 years old so I am on my ...n now. I have a collection of animals that have maybe been treated ...ng or I just got because I really wanted them. I like to think that I am ...ng them from something bad.

...ve lived all over the world but my house is in New Jersey. I live on a ...n but have no farm animals today. I have my dog Bailey, she is a Pit-... I got her just a year ago right after I left the orphanage. I adopted her ...n a shelter and she is the sweetest thing in the world. So now to the ...y... Right now I live in New Jersey. I have to take care of myself and ...dog. We have to go to the pet shop and then the supermarket to buy ...d. It's a pretty long walk to the mall. We walk through a forest and ...ugh some roads to get there. In the mall there's a supermarket, a pet ...p, a Dollar Tree and many more stores. I always stop in the Dollar Tree. ...ve walked into the supermarket I looked at my shopping list. It looked ...this: lettuce, tomato, cheese, orange juice, cereal, soda, pasta, red sauce, ...wnie mix, and an ice cube tray. I did pick up some movies like ...picable Me and Space Buddies. My total was $50. I then went over to ...pet shop and bought dog food, Christmas collars, Christmas leashes, ...aters, and Christmas toys. My total ended up being $30. Then I went to ...Dollar Tree and I got Christmas decor, micro beads, storage bins, and ...ight candles.

...had to walk all the way home. We walked through the forest and across ...reet and then we went to the travel agent. They were having a sale on ...ts to Japan after Christmas. It was $500 to fly to Japan. I walked in ...sat down with a man named Bill. He told me about all the expenses I ...ld have like having to pay extra for a dog friendly hotel. It was $10

8

journey started.

I waited weeks and weeks for it to be Christmas. I did a lot of housewor
and yard work to make sure we were ready to go to Japan. Bailey and I
were all ready to go. The house was clean the yard was pretty and we we
watching some Christmas specials. I ended up falling asleep on the couc
asked Santa for a carrying cage for Bailey and all the stuff we needed for
in her crate, which included a water bowl, a food bowl, a bed and some
treats for her. When I woke up in the morning there were two presents
under the tree. The biggest one was Bailey's carrying cage. She was only
year old but she still needed to go under the plane with the cargo. The o
present was a camera in a nice case. Bailey got her vaccines 2 weeks bef
Christmas.

We had only 3 days to go before we left for Japan and those days went
really fast. All we did was pack the rest of Bailey's stuff and then pack t
carry on. It was finally the day that we got on the plane to go to Japan.
took a taxi to the airport and then I found one of the big carts. We wen
get to in the line to check our luggage. We waited in the line for about 1
minutes. Then the man that puts the luggage on the plane asked me for
passport and plane ticket. "I am flying United Airlines to Japan." I said i
an excited voice. He put the little tag on my suitcase then he told me to
to the left and then straight to drop off Bailey.

I walked for about 2 minutes then I reached the check-in counter. The
asked me a bunch of boring questions like, "What airline are you flying?"
and "Can I see your plane ticket?" Then he asked me to take Bailey to t
green outside to let her go to the bathroom. I took her back in and then
her settled in her cage. The man put her crate with some other dogs.

I had to go through security before I could eat. I walked to security. I ha
to take off my chain and put my carry on the security table. They said I
good to go. I headed for the restaurants and I sat down to eat. The man
came and asked me what I wanted to eat? I asked for chicken for Bailey
Mac and cheese for me. I took my food to go so I could eat it on the pla

I walked towards the plane's sitting area and I sat down to play on my
phone. They started to call everybody to board the plane. I got in line ar

...ing there asked me for my plane ticket. Then after she checked it, she
...ne get on the plane. After I walked through the tunnels I got to the
...e. There was a lady counting to make sure everybody got on the plane.
...lked through a couple aisles to get to the man who was telling
...ybody where their seats were.   He showed me the way to my seat. He
...you're in the window seat.

...t down and looked outside. It was pretty dark on the plane. After a
...rt time a lady came and sat next to me. She asked me a few questions.
...wanted to know what my name was and where my parents were. I told
...my story and then she understood. A couple minutes after there was an
...ouncement that we were starting to take off. We had to fasten our
...belts and then we started moving and turning. I looked out the window
...saw the runway lights. We stopped and zoomed down the runway! As
...eft the ground I could see New York from high up. We were in the air!

It was pretty late so I was tired. I fell right asleep. When I woke up I
had an hour until we arrived in Japan. I watched a television show and
they were already announcing to buckle up your seatbelts and put any c
under the seat or on shelves up above. We started to feel the plane get
lower. I looked out my window and I could sort of see Japan. We
getting lower and lower until finally I heard the plane touch the grour
was finally in Japan!

I couldn't wait to see Bailey. The plane attendants started helping pe
off the plane. I grabbed my carry on and then I said bye to the nice lad
couldn't wait to run off the plane. When I got into the airport I could
Japan it was beautiful. I ran to the line that said luggage pickup. When I
there I was looking for luggage pickup number 5. I saw a dog and I
towards it. Bailey was in the cage and she was wagging her tail so fa
went to find my luggage. It was one of the first ones that came out. It
easy to spot my green bag. Then I looked for Bailey's bag. Her bag
pink. I got a luggage cart and put all my bags on it. I took Bailey out of
crate and put that on the cart.

Bailey and I walked through the airport. When we got outside I looked f
taxi that allowed dogs. The driver asked where we were going. I said,
Royal Hotel of Tokyo." He said it would be about 40 yen. I said, "ok
put my luggage in the back of the car and Bailey and I got in. When
started driving I asked him if he could put down the window. There v
so many stores and restaurants. When we finally got to my hotel I paid
thanked the driver. The doorman came to help me with my luggage.
inside of the Hotel was so beautiful. I went to the front desk to chec
He gave me my room key and then a Bell boy helped me with my bags
took me up to my room. It was an amazing room with great views.
said, "Hope you enjoy your room."

I started to unpack my suitcase. There was a mini kitchen and a
bedroom. I unpacked all my clothes into the drawers in my bedroo
brought some food. I put that in the kitchen with Bailey's dog food
her dog bowls. I put her bed in the lounge area. There were hooks on
wall, so I hung her leash on one. I put Bailey's sweaters in the closet
put one on her. After that I put Bailey on her leash, grabbed my book
and headed to the Lobby.

When we got downstairs I went to the front desk and asked what tin

11

pet shop to get some stuff for Bailey. He said, "ok." The pet shop is
:d the General Pet shop. "Ok," I said. In a couple minutes a taxi came
to the curb and asked where he could take me. I said, " to the General
Shop." He said, "ok, that will be ten yen". He drove me to the pet
e. Along the way there were so many colors and sights.

Pet store was huge…7floors!   The first floor was for small pets; the
ond floor was for dogs. So, I had to go up one floor. There were tons
hings for dogs. First, I went over to the collar section. They were so
: and so cheap (3 yen for a collar and 4 yen for a leash).   I bought a hot
collar and a matching leash. Then, I went over to the bandana section
I picked up some cute bandanas for Bailey. I got her a cameo one and
aristmas one for next year. I went over to the food section it looked like
' had some good food so I got 3 cans so she could try it. If she likes it
buy her more.

ent up a floor just to see what they had. They were selling mice for 2 yen
all the supplies you needed was 10 yen.   That is a whole set which
ild last an entire year. I decided I would look and see if there were any
e that I fell in love with. There was a really cute white one with brown
ts. I asked the Sales Lady if I could take the one that I wanted. She told
that he was a boy. I thanked her and she told me to pick out a carrying
: for him while she was getting him out.   I got him an orange carrying
:. She also told me I needed to get a second mouse so he wouldn't get
ly. I picked out another mouse that was a boy so they wouldn't have
les. I had to get extra food, a starter set which came with treats, a cage,
l bowl, water bottle, bedding, a wheel, and a hut. I grabbed all my stuff
went back over to the Sales Lady. She gave me the carrying cage with
2 mice in it. I put the food and the starter kit in my basket and went to
first floor to pay. My total was 28 yen.

ad to walk around with the mice, Bailey and the stuff that I bought at
pet shop, but I was very happy. I hailed a taxi to go back to the hotel.
en we got back to the hotel I put the mouse cage on the dining room
e. I filled up their water bottles and put food in their cage. The mice
e happy to be in their new home. I decided I would name the one with
wn spots Ralph and the white one, Jimmy. I left them in the dining
m and closed the cage. I asked Bailey if she wanted to go out again and
looked like she was happy after I asked. I left the room and I headed
the lobby.

After about 10 minutes we were at the park. I got out and there was a by the park. There were so many homeless cats but one just kept com up to me and Bailey. Finally, I picked her up and the cat fell asleep in lap. I thought to myself that she must be a kitten and I felt so bad for so guess what? I now have 1 dog, 2 mice, and 1 cat!

I decided to name the cat Sushi because I found her in Japan. Now I to go back to the pet shop to get some stuff for her. I hailed a taxi an asked him to go to the general pet shop. It took about 4 minutes unti got there. I got out of the taxi and walked in the pet store and headed the cat section. I got a bed, leash, collar, food, food bowl, water bowl toys. After I got those I decided to walk around. As soon as we got out I put the leash and collar on Sushi so she could walk. I was so surpr how well Bailey got along with Sushi. It was getting pretty dark so I dec to get dinner and then go back to the hotel. I passed a place that loo really nice. So I went in and ordered a plate of sushi and I watched sunset. I ate my dinner and then I had to go back to the hotel to give animals some food. I ended up walking back to the hotel. When we back the mice were in their cage. One was on the wheel. I got Bailey's f bowl out and put some of the new Japanese dog food and the chicken I got her at the airport. Then I put Sushi's cat food in her bowl. Once were all fed, I started to set up the beds for all my pets. I went into bedroom to bed. I was so tired.

next day was so beautiful outside. I saw all my pets. They were all [ly]ing on their beds. I went into the kitchen and I made myself a bowl of [Luc]ky Charms that I brought from my house in America. I went to get my [bac]k bag so I could go out with my animals. I told them to come so I [coul]d take them to the harbor. I could not wait to go on a whale watching [trip]. I really wanted to see some whales because they are one of my favorite [ani]mals. I took Sushi's leash and then I took Bailey's leash. I put them on [thei]r leashes, filled up the mouse bowls, and headed out the door. I walked [dow]n to the street and then toward the harbor. I walked past a lot of stores [and] a lot of restaurants before reaching this huge boat. I walked over to [read] the sign. It read, "Whale Watching tickets sold here".

[The]re were 4 people in line in front of me. I was waiting for about 10 [min]utes before I finally got to the front of the line. There was a man [stan]ding that asked me, "How many people?" I said, "One cat, one dog [and] me." He said my total was 12 yen and he handed me my tickets. I went [to s]et on the boat and the man told me we had to wait 10 minutes until we [wer]e leaving. So, I waited and before long he was calling everybody to get [on t]he boat. I walked towards the boat. I handed him my ticket and he put [a ho]le in it.

[I w]alked onto the boat. I walked down to the bottom level to get a really [goo]d view. I thought I could touch the whales if I sat on the bottom level. [The]re was a strange section in the bottom of the boat which was very dark. [I sl]owly walked over and I saw huge nets. There was a door that read, ["Pri]vate". I looked at the door then I walked in slowly. There were huge [net]es and the biggest butcher table in the world. I thought to myself they [are] killing whales! Before I could even finish thinking I heard a voice [I sc]am. "Come on boys lets go get the nets ready, and make sure people [don]'t see you". I ran to a corner and sat really close to Bailey and Sushi. [The]re was a curtain so I pulled it over us. I heard someone come in.

[I w]as so scared. I peeked a little bit and I saw two men screaming at each [oth]er. One was ordering the other man around. He was saying, "Get the [net]s ready and get some more knifes!" You could tell by the tone of his [voic]e that he was extremely angry. I felt the boat start moving and I heard [the] horn. I peeked out again. The men were by the window waiting for [som]ething. I think they were getting ready to catch a whale or a dolphin.

[I w]atched them for about 14 minutes until we got out to the open sea and

heard a lot of screaming. People were yelling, "whales, whales. I s
pod of whales. Look there' a bunch of them Mommy!" I peeked out
all the men were looking out the window. There was a hole in the boa
they could reach out. I was thinking to myself what can I do to help
whales? I wanted to help them so bad. Well I took karate lessons 5 y
ago. Hmmm…what can I do?

I was still thinking about what I could do. There were nets all over the
floor so how could I help the whales? The men were all looking out the
hole. I could see a whale close to the ship. The men were trying to thro
the net over the whale but I didn't think that would work. They were
getting closer and closer to catching the whale. Then out of nowhere, I w
not able to control myself. It was as if I became a Ninja with my emotio
I ran up to the men and kicked one man in the head and he fell down. T
other men came running at me. I jumped up on the table so I could eith
jump from them or kick them. One man jumped on the table and swun
kick at me. I ducked to avoid his kick and spotted a metal pipe. I grabb
onto it and started swinging. I kicked and kicked until all three men wer
on the ground. I thought to myself I only have one more man to take
down. He was standing there staring at me. I swung and he ducked. T
I jumped down and we started fighting. He swung a kick and I kicked b
Finally, I did the final kick and he fell to the ground.

The whale was stuck in the net, and the net was on his back. I quickly g
a knife and cut the net. The whale was almost free and then I cut the la
piece. The whale was free! He swam up close to me. I told him to nev
swim by these kinds of boats again and then I kissed him on his head. F
looked at me and swam away. I looked at Bailey and Sushi and they just
stared back at me like I was AWESOME! I walked over towards my
animals, picked up their leashes and walked out of the room. I sat down
rest and thought wow I am very proud of myself!

at sea, we saw a lot of whales. I kept checking on the men every 5
utes to make sure they were not awake. I was wondering what I was
g to do about them because I'm not always going to be in Japan to
ect the whales. I looked around and there was a girl who was just
ng all alone looking out the window. She looked like she was from
n but I wasn't sure. I went over to sit next to her. She was the only
r person on the bottom floor. As I walked towards her she stared at
and then she said "spot here will sit? She sounded like she didn't know
to speak English. She looked at me and then I sat down.

ced her if she had any interest in animals. She started laughing like the
ver was obvious and I should have known. I looked at her like I had no
 why she was laughing. Finally, when she calmed down, she told me
 much she loved them. After awhile she was talking my ear off. She
n't shy anymore (and she spoke English very well). She told me her
ie was Sakura. She started telling me about all the adventures she had
animals. She told me about all her dogs and all the rest of her pets. It
like she was Miss Animal. I thought to myself she is the perfect person
elp me save the whales when I leave. I asked her if she could help me
 the whales. She said, "I would love to help save whales!" I was very
oy about that. We discussed how she was going to help. We thought it
ld be good for her to take pictures of the people hurting whales and
 put on the pictures on the internet so more people would be aware of
problem and could help to stop the killing.

r awhile we went back into the little room to check on the men. The
 were still there but they were on the ground asleep. We saw three
e whales. There was a blue whale, a gray whale and a humpback whale.
y were all beautiful creatures. I took a video recording of the gray whale
 the humpback whale with the camera I got on Christmas. It was so
itiful. I took so many pictures of them and got some really good shots.

boat was almost in port and Sakura and I decided to spend the day
ther. The plan was to go shopping, hit the beach, and then go out for a
 Sushi dinner. What really made my day is she told me she wanted to
a new pet at the pet shop. She lived by herself and she was going to
 me to see her other pets. Then I was going to take her to my hotel
n to introduce her to Jimmy and Ralph. It was going to be a great day!

got off the boat and started walking towards the road so that we could

sitting near the window looking out at all the sights. I was in the mi
and Sakura was next to me. In a few minutes we arrived at the hotel
went inside. I showed her Jimmy and Ralph and she wanted to hold on
them. She picked out Jimmy and held him. It was so cute she loved l
She wanted to hold him for the whole time she was visiting which was
about 10 minutes because we had the whole day planned. Sakura put Jin
back in his cage and we started walking out. She asked if she could ·
Bailey and I said "okay."

Our first stop was the pet shop. It was the same pet shop where I bou
Ralph and Jimmy (my two mice). We walked into the store and v
upstairs to the floor with the mice. I walked her over and showed
where I found my mice. The same lady was still there and she asked
she could help us. We told her we were looking for the single mouse.
took us over to pick one out but they were all so cute running around.
Sales lady said to pick out the mouse we wanted. Sakura decoded
wanted 4 of them. I thought she was crazy! I asked her how she was g
to take care of all of them? She said, "I have no idea, but I found a wa
care for 14 other pets." Wow!!! Sakura, now has 18 pets including her
mice! We picked out a caring cage and the rest of the stuff she nee
When we were in line, we noticed the store was having a sale on Betta
They were 20 yen for three, so picked a pink one, a blue one, and a g
one.

After the pet store we left to go back to the harbor. We wanted to
Bailey swim in the water. Sakura asked me when I was flying bac
America. I told her I was leaving on a 5:30 flight. It was only 1:00 so
had some time to go back to the harbor. The water was beautiful. B
and Sushi were running around on the beach. I started looking for s
and I found some really pretty ones. It was about 3:30 when we left
beach. I needed to get back to the hotel to get all of my stuff pac
Sakura hailed a taxi and we headed back to the hotel. She said she w
stay with me until I went to the airport. I packed all of my things and
it was time to go to the airport. Her mice were in her hands the entire
we were at the hotel.

walked down stairs to the Lobby I became really sad. I was sad
ause I was going to miss Sakura so much. As I got into the cab she was
ing. I realized I didn't give her a hug goodbye. I jumped out and gave
a big hug. I got back in the taxi and the man started driving away.

airport was really nice. Before I knew it, I was on the plane. I was sad
e leaving Japan. I had a window seat and my fish and my mice were
me on the plane. As we were taking off I was looking down at Japan
it was so beautiful. About 2 hours had past, with 6hrs to go, when the
t made an announcement. He said, "We are so sorry but we will be
ping in the Greek National Airport." I heard a lot of disappointed
le say, "Oh, great we're going to be stuck there." I decided I would
get angry because there was nothing I could do about it.

r we landed, I walked out. I was not disappointed at all because Greece
really beautiful. It was cold outside, but it was very nice. I was actually
ty excited because this was my first time to Greece. We were delayed in
ece for 2 days. It was so amazing! There were oceans, a bunch of
urants and stores. I walked outside and hailed a taxi and I asked where
vere. He responded "Mykonos Greece." I asked him if he knew of any
friendly hotels in the area. "Yes, there's one about 30 minutes away
d the Grand Hotel" he responded. Luckily, the airline was paying for
ybody's hotel.

n we got to the Grand Hotel I paid the taxi driver and walked in. I
d the concierge for my room key and then walked upstairs. I was
ying Bailey's kennel, my fish, and my mice. Sushi was tied to Bailey's
nel. The room was amazing with a great view. On the bed I found a
of fun local stuff to do. I looked at it and it had the dates of this week.
id there was a Greek market today and I thought maybe we can check
that or a festival. I decided to take Bailey to the Greek market and
ted outside with the map. I followed the map and after awhile I saw the
ket. It was filled with animals tied to ropes, clothing and other antique
s. As we were walking, people were yelling, "Donkeys get your donkey,
20 euros." "Wow!, I said to Bailey, I love donkeys."

18

man screamed at her and said something in Greek. He apologized to m
The donkey tried to follow us. It looked like she was scared of her own
looked at her owner and without thinking I told the man I would like to
buy the donkey. I handed him the euros, we shook hands and the donk
started licking my hand as we walked away.

Many of the local people looked really sad and depressed. One woma
came up to me and asked me to buy her pigs. She said she could no lon
care for them and she needed the money. I asked her how much she
wanted for them and she told me 20 euros for 15 pigs! She said she wa
to find them a good home. I had to help all of them, so I agreed to buy
them. We shook hands and off we went. Bailey and I now have 15 pig
mice, 1 cat, 1 donkey and fish. Wow!

We kept walking through the markets. All the pigs looked so happy no
because the woman wasn't able to properly care for them. They were v
small and only babies. I wanted to ride my donkey. On her back were
storage sacks connected to a saddle. I was able to put the baby pigs in a
basket. I found a market stand that was selling baskets and blankets so I
bought them. I also found hand knitted little baby booties. I bought 2
of booties and 2 hats for each baby pig since it was cold. When I put th
booties on the pigs, they were so happy. I also bought blankets for Bail
and Sushi. I placed the pigs in the basket and attached them to the sack
the donkey. Sushi was able to snuggle into one of the pouches and Bail
was on my lap. I sat on the donkey and we walked through town. I not
people staring at me like I was crazy. I didn't care because I had a great
saving animals!

It started to get dark and then it started to rain. I decided it was best to
head back to the hotel. As we walked back, all my animals fell asleep.
When we got back to the hotel, I realized that I needed a Farm Room. I
asked the front desk clerk and she was able to switch my room. I went
get my things and followed the Bell Boy to the farm room. It was a very
cool room with hay and 2 beds. I closed the door and looked through t
things I purchased at the market. I put the fish and the mice on the tabl
They were sound asleep. I carefully put Bailey on my bed (she was so
tired). I put Sushi on the same bed as Bailey. I put the pigs on the hay

ınd for the donkey. I laid down and fell asleep.

ıe morning, the pigs were running around in their little booties
ealing. I figured they must be hungry. I went in the fridge and there was
ı and lettuce. I gave lettuce to the pigs and donkey and gave Bailey and
ıi their canned food. I fed the mice grain and fed the fish their special
ł. The phone rang. It was the airline telling me that the plane was ready
.y a day early. I was a little disappointed to leave Greece, but happy to
.eading home to America.

ıs very excited to see my new animals playing on my farm. I packed my
ı and got the donkey ready to help get us to the airport. I put the
key saddle and his storage sacks on his back. I put the pigs in their
:et. I grabbed my suit case and tied it to the donkey. I put Bailey, Sushi,
the mice in the back and put the fish on my lap. We grabbed the map
headed for the airport. The people at the airport took Bailey, the
key and the pigs to put them in crates. I walked with the mice, fish, and
ıi to the plane. The plane was leaving at 12:00 it was 11:51. Oh my
ı! I ran to the flight and gave the lady my plane ticket. I ran in and I
·d a man say, "Hello and welcome to Indian airways." Indian Airlines?
d him that I was going to New York. The man said, "Sorry, this plane
»ing to India first." I sighed and then relaxed. There was nothing I
d do so off to India we went!

It was the next day and we were landed in India. I walked to the receptio and asked when the next flight was to New York. They man said, "Midnight tonight, but it will be stopping in Switzerland for 1 night befc landing in New York". I decided to take that flight and explore Switzer. for the day. He handed me my plane ticket. I thanked him and headed towards the exit.

In a special pickup area, I was so excited to see Bailey, the pigs, the don Sushi, my mice and all my other animals. I loaded up the donkey with th animals and found a map. I was very excited to explore India. We walk into the streets and came across an open market. There was one stand t was selling goats. They were very cute, but were very sad. They spent th days in the hot market and didn't have any open space to play or eat gra I wanted to help them, but thought I already had so many animals. As I tried to ride away, I looked back and one of the baby goats was looking me (baby goats are called 'kids'). Bailey was also looking back and forth between me and the baby goat. I knew she thought we should help the goat. I went back and asked the man how much for the goats. He told that 1 goat was 3 rupees. I looked in my pocket and I had 10 rupees. I said, "Ok I'll take the goat."

He put the goat with my other animals on the donkey. The goat was so cute and looked so happy. I knew I had made the right decision buying him. We rode around India for about 2 hours. It was amazingly beautif saw rivers, trees, beaches and many more pretty things. It was getting d and I was starting to get hungry. I started to look for a restaurant to eat and found one that smelled amazing. I left the animals outside where I could see them. It was around 8:00 and the plan was to eat and then he to the airport. I had no idea where I was, so I was a little scared I woul lost and miss my flight. As I ate, I watched the sunset. It was so amazi

I finished dinner and headed towards the airport. I looked at the map a was happy that I was going the right way. The signs on the road read, "Airport ahead." After passing about 50 airport signs I arrived at the airport. They took all my animals even my goat and mice and fish to pu under the plane. I walked to my gate and checked with the Flight Attenc that this was the right gate to go to Switzerland and then to New York. said it was and I waited until they started to board the plane. I got on, s down then feel asleep.

ing breakfast. I don't like airplane food but ate it anyway since I was so
gry. After awhile I heard the Pilot ask everyone to take their seats and
en their seatbelts. They made the announcement in several different
uages. I felt the plane going downward and also saw the plane leaning
n side to side. I could see Switzerland and where we were landing. It
ed really rustic and there was a lot of farm land.

As soon as we landed I grabbed my carry-on bag and got off the plane. I was so excited to see Bailey and all the other animals. I ran to the baggage claim. They were all there waiting for me. I grabbed them and my suitcase. Then I went over to the place where you can get carts for your luggage. I quickly put everything on the cart and ran to the passport checking section. There was a huge line. I sighed then I ran into the line that looked the shortest. I was 4th in the line. I waited and waited and then finally I stepped onto the red line and herd the lady say "Next." I was excited because that was me. I quickly walked over to her booth. She asked for my passport. I gave it to her and then walked over to the exit.

As I was leaving the airport I saw a taxi driver holding up a card with my last name. He had a large van so all of my animals could fit. He grabbed my fish and put them in the back. He put my mice, Sushi, and my donkey in the back. The back was huge so it fit all of them. Bailey and my pigs went to the front with me. The pigs were squealing and the donkey was snorting. It sounded like a zoo!!

When we arrived to my hotel, it looked amazing from the outside. The hotel was a little farm house. I walked inside and saw the reception lady. She was wearing a little white dress with different colored fabrics on top. She asked how she could help me. I told her about the animals and that I needed a room where animals were allowed. She asked me what type of animals I had. I told her I had a dog, a donkey, small pigs, fish and mice. She said she had a mini-farm shed and showed me to my room. The taxi driver unloaded all my stuff and animals to the mini farm shed. When we got outside it looked like a little farm village. It had a mini farm and 2 pastures. I walked inside there was a bed, a little television and a back door leading to the mini farm area. It was the most amazing hotel I've ever stayed at. I went inside and started unpacking. I put my fish on a table next to my mice and picked up my pigs and walked outside. I put their grain in a little wooden box that was hanging off the side of the fence. Then I brought my donkey out to the second pasture and put his carrots and lettuce in the box. I shut the gate and went back inside.

The flight to America was the next morning so I wanted to see as much age with Bailey and Sushi's leads in my hands. I went to the front desk asked them for a map. The Receptionist said there was a Cow Desalpe g on in town. She said that dinner was at 6:00 so I headed out of the l to find the Desalpe.

llowed the map, but got very lost. When we were walking down a small et, Bailey pulled me towards a man's yard. There was a shed and I heard ething. I looked around and then slowly walked in. We saw a bunch of bunnies. They were so cute. There was a man there and he said that I ed him. I apologized and asked him where he got so many bunnies? told me that the big ones had babies and he was raising them for food. en I looked at the baby rabbits I knew I had to save them. I asked him could buy them from him. He said he would sell them to me for 10 ss Francs. I quickly agreed and bought all of them including the big s for 30 Swiss Francs. He gave me a carrying case and gave me ctions to the town festival.

walked out and as soon as we got into town I heard bells ringing and I d hoofs hitting the ground. I watched lots of cows wearing big bells decorated with flowers walk past. The Cow Desalpe was amazing! en the parade was finished I decide to go back to the hotel. I asked the eptionist what was Switzerland's most popular animal. She told me it the Swiss cow. I asked her if she knew of any farmers that sold them. told me there was a farm right down the road. I quickly ran to the farm found the farmer. I asked him if he raised the cows for milk. He said id, but also raised them for food. There was a baby cow that he said going to be sold to a restaurant. The baby cow was very cute with vn, black and white spots. I asked him if I could buy him instead. He if he sold the cow to me he would also have to sell me his mother since vas still too young. I told him about my other animals and my farm k in America and the farmer agreed to sell them to me for 150 Swiss ics. I gave him the money and he gave me a rope for the cows to get n back to the hotel. When I got back to the room I put my cows in the ure with my donkey. I made sure every animal had food and then went inner. Dinner was really good. I ordered pasta with red sauce. When I e back to my room all my animals were asleep. I got into bed and fell ep. The next morning I got all my stuff ready and put all the animals in

I was very excited to be going home back to the USA!

We arrived to the airport and the lady asked about all of my animals. I g
her all of the paperwork and my ticket and headed to security. I had to
take off my shoes and my jewelry. After security I went to the dining ar
and ate some more pasta. I heard the lady announce that all passengers
going to New York had to head to Gate 34. I ran to gate 34 and gave th
Attendant my boarding pass. I ran through 5 tunnels to get to the actua
plane. I sat down and fell asleep even though I was so excited. When I
woke up there was only 1 hour left. I ate my breakfast, and prepared fo
landing. We landed and I was so excited to be home. I was one step av
from a new life on my farm with Bailey and all my animals!

et the taxi driver at the airport and we filled the truck with all of my
nals and my luggage.   I was so excited to show my new animal family
: new and safe home! When we arrived, the animals jumped from the
k and started to run around the farm. They were so excited stepping
 their new lives and I was so happy to live a life full of happiness with
ny animals.

EAR LATER....

e on my farm and remember the best memories from my travels. Sushi
nd a friend and had a baby kitten. I named her Sakura after my friend
n Japan. Speaking of Sakura, I stay in touch with her. She recently sent
a letter with pictures of her and the whales she has been saving. Life
been great for Bailey and me!

ABOUT THE AUTHOR

My name is Brianna and I am from America. I love animals and love
help them.

My favorite animals are dogs, whales, and pigs. I have three dogs: Ruf
Rosie, and Jack and three rabbits: Cotton Tail, Coffee Bean and Fluff-t

I live with my mother, father, my sister, Alexis, and my brother, Zacha

Made in the USA
Lexington, KY
03 April 2014

He responded with that lilting, sustained "Ooh, okay" I've heard from nearly everybody I've ever told I was pre-med. That change in tone is usually accompanied by some type of head tilt or soft, presumptive smile.

"Impressive," he said.

"Yeah, well, don't be too impressed just yet. I dropped organic chemistry, biology—everything that would remotely qualify as a science prerequisite—and took some kind of lit class or philosophy or fine arts studio instead. Every quarter last year. I almost declared myself a theater major."

"Theater," he said. "Hmm. I could see you being an actor."

"I was in a play junior year of high school. A musical actually. I even *sang*."

"No way. What show?"

"*The Wizard of Oz*—and don't laugh—I was the Tin Woodman."

"Well, he is the gay one."

"Fuck you," I said, although it came out sounding like I wanted to.

"You're clearly heartless."

Hutch had made the same joke when I told him that story.

I found myself confessing a surprising amount of blatantly honest information about my academic tribulations. I told Gavin my plan had been to go to

Emory or Vanderbilt, but I fucked up my grades my junior year in high school. After all those years of my mother clawing our way into an expensive boarding school, I ended up at a public state university. I told him that I predicted eventually wearing my mom down to accept the fact that I was probably going to graduate with a bachelor's in art history or ancient languages or some other disappointingly unmarketable humanities degree. She'd probably compromise her expectations somewhat, enough to start harping on finance, which would lead me to change my major to English just to spite her.

Gavin was eager to relate a similar sob story. His family had spent a fortune on tutors trying to wedge him into Pace Academy, where all his older siblings had gone. But thanks to mild dyslexia and serious alcohol abuse, he barely graduated from Norcross High School with a GPA just above average enough to get into UGA.

Encouraged by our commiseration, he segued into telling me about how he'd taken "what we'd been through together" as a sign. He confessed to wanting to meet a guy that he could actually date "for, like, forever," and it had never happened. Until me. I had no idea how almost getting arrested having sex in my car had not been a sign *deterring* him from wanting to spend more time with me, but he had indeed come to the opposite conclusion. So opposite, in fact, he claimed it was a serendipitous event that had prompted him to confront the fact that he was gay. He wanted to come out of the closet. And he wanted to do it by taking me as a date to a fraternity party.

I expressed to him that I was worried this might be

too large a step, too big a statement, or too challenging an environment for a first time going on a date in public with another guy.

"I'd personally rather this did not end with a mob of drunken frat boys screaming 'faggot' at us," I said.

Gavin laughed. "You think they're going to try to beat the shit out of us? These are my brothers. That's not gonna happen."

"No, I know that's not gonna happen. You misunderstand my concern. I'm not worried about losing a fight; I'm worried about losing *it*. I don't respond well to being bullied."

"Are you being serious?"

"Deadly."

I heard him sigh on the other end of the line. "Come on," he said. "Go with me."

Considering that he had his heart set on my participating in this milestone of his, and considering that I was "honored," in the most awkward way possible, and considering that my hesitations were mostly lip service—I had tried to take a guy as a date to my senior prom and the school refused to sell us tickets or let us in—and considering that I didn't even know these people and was secretly looking forward to it...I reluctantly agreed to go.

But I kept my biggest concern to myself: that, regardless of where we went, I might be showing up on the arm of a guy wearing those regrettable white jeans.

"So," I tried to sound casual while coming right out and asking, "what do you think you're gonna wear?"

FIVE

I got a strange call at work. I had never received a personal call there before, as it was expressly forbidden. I sneaked around and dialed out once in a while, just briefly, but I never gave anyone the number. Not even my mother. Especially not her; she was the most likely person to use it.

Getting any kind of phone call at all while you were on the sales floor was unusual; that my manager put it through and told me over the intercom to take it was nothing short of troubling.

It had to be bad news.

It was worse. Some kind of detective. Agent Wood from the G.B.I. He said he wanted to ask me some questions about the burglaries at the shops on South Lumpkin. I didn't know he meant right then, over the phone.

"Mr. Stewart, do you have any information regarding

the identity of the suspect seen entering and leaving the Hearth & Home Gift Shop via the rooftop of the Harriet Building?"

"The what? I don't know where the Harriet Building is."

"The Harriet Building is the Stein Properties apartment building on South Lumpkin that also houses their management office."

Ah.

I told him, like I told Officer Brody, that I had a friend who lived in the building, but I had no idea that there had been break-ins. It was just a convenient parking space to me—and apparently a really bad coincidence.

Agent Wood wanted to know the name of my friend in the building. All I cared about was that my story checked out, and I had already blurted it out to Officer Brody, so I didn't hesitate to tell him. "Charlotte O'Brien." Stuttering a bit on the *sh* sound, I almost said "Sugar." I felt like he thought I was making it up. He asked me to spell her last name.

My boss came out of his office and started walking toward me. I whispered the letters a little fiercely and told Agent Wood that I was at work and really needed to go. I told him we weren't allowed to take personal calls. I'm sure it sounded like I was making an excuse to get off the phone. I doubted he cared, but he let me go pretty quickly. But he also told me that he would be "following up." He said it in a friendly tone, which made it seem all the more menacing. I honestly didn't know if he was genuinely unconcerned, if it was just a boring part of his job, or if he was intentionally fucking with my mind.

For my boss, I made a big show of hanging up. He watched me and then ducked back into his office.

I wandered around, idly straightening hangers and refolding sweaters. My hearing was muffled and my heart was racing. For some reason, I started having all these anxious visions of Officer Brody knocking on Charlotte's door or Agent Wood calling her, and her claiming that she had never heard of me before in her life. I don't know why I thought that. I guess probably because it was the worst, yet entirely feasible thing, I could imagine happening at that moment. I could see Charlotte either protecting Mickey or saying something unpredictable, like that she didn't know me, for absolutely no specific reason. And she was always so practiced and artfully fake. They'd probably think she was sweet as pie and buy whatever suck-up smiling line she fed them.

The lady working in the Boys' Department came over to relieve me so that I could take my lunch hour.

I had no appetite. In the food court, I picked at one of the meatballs at the end of a Sbarro sub and then went outside to chain-smoke for the rest of my break.

On the outskirts of the parking lot, I found a doughnut-shaped patch of sprinkler-misted grass and concrete curb under a pine tree—landscaping remnants that could exist only in the asphalt sprawl around a mall. It was so humid. I felt disgusting in my dress clothes. I yanked off my tie, stripped out of my button-down shirt, folded my suit jacket into a pillow, and laid down right there. I'm sure I looked like a homeless crazy person. I wondered vaguely if it was illegal to lie on a parking lot island, but what was mall security when the G.B.I. already suspected you of burglarizing high-end boutiques? Why was the G.B.I. involved, anyway? Somehow it all made me less concerned about committing other crimes. I had clearly already crossed some Line.

I found a giant cloud in the sky as pretty as a colorless beehive of cotton candy and decided to try to see if I could bust it up with my mind.

Talking to that detective had made me realize how little I trusted Charlotte. Although I knew not to even mention Mickey's existence to any kind of investigator, I had not been so quick to protect her, had I? I didn't really care if Charlotte was troubled or if she gave Mickey away, as long as she corroborated our acquaintance. That was what she was—an acquaintance. Maybe one of the most interesting acquaintances I'd ever made. But she didn't really qualify as a friend.

It struck me how little you have to like people to find them interesting.

I took long drags off my cigarette and exhaled smoke in forced streams toward the cloud above me. It seemed like, given enough time to travel the distance, they could reach their target. I thought about calling on any spirits that might be around me and asking them for help. But it just didn't feel like there would be any ghosts in a mall parking lot.

What if the clouds literally were spirits? Life can't exist without water. What if water and life force are composed of the same underlying material? Tears and sweat and the electricity of thoughts and feelings that animate it all. What if that infinitesimal—but reportedly measurable—*something* that leaves the body is an exhalation of the soul? The dying breath, a sigh that rides molecules of vapor into the sky.

I wasn't sure if my efforts were tinting the underbelly of the cloud a bit gray or if I were responsible for the hazy edges that seemed to be tearing away in small wisps. I didn't have enough break time or cigarettes left to confirm it. I definitely felt different when I went back inside. A bit lightheaded. But not in an entirely unpleasant way.

SIX

The new phone in the cottage rang for the first time. Charlotte invited me to go over on Wednesday and spend the afternoon with her. She said she wanted it to be "just us."

I had worked out my notice at Macy's. School was starting the next Monday. Every day, people were arriving back in town, and there were bound to be a lot of parties that coming weekend. I had picked up the keys to the cottage from the new landlord and driven my boxes over from the apartment. The power was on and the phone was working, but my roommates Alexandra and Gabrielle wouldn't arrive until Friday.

There was really nothing to do but kill time, so I said, "Sure."

"Wonderful, Sugar! I'm going to fix us a beautiful little luncheon. Filet mignon with a salad and baguette. Why don't you pick us up a bottle of merlot?"

Us. I translated that to mean "pick *me* up a bottle of merlot." She seemed unable—or unwilling—to retain the fact that I did not drink. Or maybe it was some complex shame that keeps an alcoholic from acknowledging that she's drinking alone.

I hesitated before parking in my usual space-that-wasn't-a-space beside the Dumpster. I could feel surveillance cameras trained on it. I recalled Officer Brody telling me he couldn't think of any reason to catch me here again. Surely lightning wouldn't strike twice, but I couldn't bring myself to test it. There really were no decent alternatives in that neighborhood other than slots reserved for shoppers. Instead, I parked at the Bottle Shop and went in to get the wine. It seemed at least semi-legitimate to leave my car there, and the worst that could happen would be getting towed.

Charlotte's meal was actually amazing. For all her *Southern Living* airs and affectations, she really could cook. I knew her well enough to be sure to tell her that I thought so.

"Oh, Sugar! Just means the world to me that you enjoyed it."

I carried our plates to the sink, but Charlotte insisted that we leave the cleanup for later. We took our drinks into the living room—my sweet tea, her third glass of wine—and settled into the same spots we occupied that first time we hung out: on the love seats across from each other. Charlotte wore a white men's dress shirt with the sleeves rolled up and unbuttoned to reveal a lace bra, this time over a pair of men's jeans widely cuffed to her calves. She'd chosen pearls over the flapper beads. She proffered a cigarette on the end of a long black holder for me to light.

"Whoa, that's new." I said, admiring the holder as I dug out a cheap plastic Bic. "Where did that come from?"

She maintained eye contact with me as she inhaled. "Isn't it delicious?" Smoke poured out around her words. She extended her arm, appraising it lovingly, treating me to a side pose like a figure in an Erté print. "I mentioned to Mickey that I'd always wanted one of these, and he found it down at the Hearth & Home. Little shop right here in that converted house at the other end of the building. Picked it up for me."

"That was generous of him," I said, even though I was thinking *Shit. There it is: my connection to these alleged burglaries.* "Where is Mickey, by the way?"

Her eyes narrowed in a cruel pout, and she flapped her hand in a slow, dismissive wave. "We'll get to him in a minute." She looked around as if she were evaluating the temperature or the light in the room and then got off the couch. "Actually, let's move out onto the screened porch."

Low charcoal clouds floated toward us from downtown. Charlotte stared out into the distance for most of the cigarette before resuming her instructions for making storms, right where she'd left off. No preamble, no segue.

"Usually, it's a cumulative thing. A bunch of energy

coming together from people who don't even know that they've projected it. Just releasing frustration out into the world. Then somebody like me can come along and sculpt it a bit. Give it a shape, a density, an intensity, a little timing. Well, actually, the timing is one of the hardest parts to get right, but... trying to explain that is a whole other can of worms. Let me come back to timing, okay?"

"Sure," I said.

"Tapping into the power is not hard if you're just getting rid of energy. Letting shit out. It's easier than most people realize. Directing it, controlling it—that's the true test. I hope you realize that putting it back is pretty much impossible."

"I imagine it would be."

"Sometimes you can even tell who a storm belongs to. We each have our own style. Now, for instance; take that one coming in right there. Sugar, I don't know who she is, but she lives out on the northeast end of town toward Winterville, and she must be just goddamned miserable. Never a bit of wind or lightning or the music of thunder—just these low, slow, sad, hot, gray clouds that spit the fattest drops. The kind you can run through and dodge. I don't know who she is, but I know her storms. I sit here and watch them come through a couple times a month. I actually like to use hers as a base for my own. I don't have to do as much work. She's sending over all this bulk but just not doing anything with it. No drama. No show!"

There was a rhythm to her words. Long, slow breaths in and out. And when she raised her voice at the end of her long, run-together speech—"No show!"—the sky cracked open in a flash of lightning. Thunder was the period. She cackled at the seemingly effortless choreography of her spectacle.

And then it began to rain again. Sheets of rain that came in sideways, cut by the screens into spray so strong it drove us back inside.

She stayed near the French doors looking out at the storm. For the first time since I'd met her, she spoke softly. As if she were rehearsing lines to herself. I stood close behind her, straining to catch her words.

"All spells have a basic recipe. Each has to contain some form of all the sacred elements. The candle flame of fire, the bodies of our earthly lives, the water of our tears. And the air? The wind is the voice, the rage of expression, squeezed through the harp of the throat. People yelling at each other. Wordless screams. The kind where you can't tell if they're making love or killing each other. Babies crying. Roaring laughter. Thousands of people way over there in Sanford Stadium cheering on the Georgia Bulldogs."

"Do you think the ghosts have anything to do with it?" I asked.

She jerked around as if she'd forgotten I was there. "You know, it has crossed my mind that it could be the spirits executing our intentions for us. Or at least helping."

"Why would they do that?" I asked.

"Because they feel connected to us. They want to participate in some way, and weather might be the only thing they can manage. Think about it: spirits manipulate electricity, and they'll pull together some small molecules in the air if the energy is present. Dust. Water vapor. Something smoky and transparent."

"Why are you telling me all this?" I asked.

"There's something about you. I sensed it that first night you came over. I don't quite have the words for it. But you're on the verge of figuring it out, aren't you?"

"I'm not sure I know what you mean," I said.

"You know, honestly, I really just wanted to tell somebody. I wanted to show somebody what I can do. Somebody who might get it. And you do."

I raised an eyebrow and shrugged. I didn't want to interrupt her. I was hoping she'd say more.

She sighed. "I'm not going to be here much longer."

"You're leaving town? What about grad school?"

She smiled and shook her head like she felt sorry for me.

"You're gonna give up this apartment?" I asked.

"Oh, I'm not the one giving up, Sugar. My parents are giving up. On me. Daddy's finally called my bluff. Let's just say, with everything else that's been happening lately, it looks like maybe God is trying to tell me something. I've run out my time." She pulled the stub of her burning cigarette out of its long holder. She walked over to the glass coffee table, stabbed the butt into the full ashtray, and laid the holder carefully beside it.

"And whether I stay or not—don't say anything to him yet; I plan to talk to him tonight, and I shouldn't be telling you before I tell him, but—I'm breaking up with Mickey."

I nodded and chewed on my lip. I wasn't surprised to hear that.

She started ticking off complaints by bending back the fingers of her left hand with her right. "He has stolen from me. Pawned family heirlooms. Taken cash right out of my pocketbook. He's talked me into loans he's never gonna pay back. We've been fighting over money since the moment I met him. And he hits me."

"What?" I sputtered in outrage. "No. Come on, now."

She held up her hand to shush me. "I don't even want to get into all that right now. Doesn't even matter anymore. It's over. I can't have the police showing up at my door, calling my phone all hours of the day and night, asking questions about some series of burglaries. They said they're looking for somebody who's getting into windows from the roof."

I winced. "Yeah, some investigator called me at work and asked me about that."

She snorted in disgust. "Well, you and I both know who that has to be."

"I didn't tell them anything, though," I said. "Did you?"

Her shoulders slumped with exaggerated exhaustion. "He's a sweet boy. But thieving and drug dealing?" She looked at me as if begging me to convince her it wasn't true. "He hasn't been right since he fell on his head. Doesn't think straight anymore. Makes bad decisions. Worse, anyway. He's gonna get caught. And he's not gonna get caught here, if I can help it." She pointed at the floor. "I'm not having the police come in here and drag some guy out of my bed in handcuffs. Thinking I'm involved."

"I get it," I said. I did.

She pressed her hand to her forehead. She cast around for something to grab, something meaningful to do, and settled on bussing the drink glasses and the overflowing ashtray. She regarded me sadly, the glasses clutched precariously between the fingers of one hand, the crystal ashtray leaning out of the limp grip of the other. She didn't notice the tiny gray flakes of ash sifting down the front of her shirt.

"You should probably leave before Mickey shows up," she said, already walking into the kitchen.

Left standing there in the middle of the room, I could choose between simply fleeing on her cue or trying to release a million pieces of opinion she wasn't likely to hear. I clapped my sides in surrender and offered my empty palms to her back. "Okay."

I heard her deposit the glasses in the sink and bang the ashtray into the garbage can. Then she reappeared to guide me toward the front door.

"Before you go, Sugar, I do want to give you something."

She removed a sweater box wrapped in white paper from the small entry table. When I took it from her, something rolled around against the cardboard inside, a faint snare drum sound.

"What's this?" I smiled at her.

"Don't open it now," she said. "I don't want to get too emotional before he gets here. Just some things I wanted you to have. You won't need an explanation. Just promise me you'll wait until you've heard that I've left town. I always leave that lamp on the credenza turned on because it lights up the French doors to the porch from inside. If you drive by and see that's not on, you'll know I'm gone."

I found myself swept along, already out in the hallway. "So, am I not going to see you again?"

She waved my question away but didn't look me in the eye. "Oh, Sugar. I'm probably just being maudlin. You'll bump into me tomorrow morning down there at the gas station buying cigarettes and rain all over my whole dramatic exit." She laughed in that simultaneously convincing and preposterous way of hers and playfully pushed my shoulder. "You run along and let me fix my face before Mickey shows up. Go on now."

I looked back up at her a few times as I stumped down the stairs. She watched me until I was out of sight.

I put her gift into the trunk of my car. I was tempted

to just go ahead and open it, but I hated to spoil the magic of whatever timing she'd intended. Because of all the people I knew who wished they lived in some kind of cinematic fantasy, she was the only one who actually tried to make it a reality. And, more times than not, she came awfully close to pulling it off.

SEVEN

Thursday night Mickey was waiting for me when I pulled in at the cottage.

"Sugar and I broke up," he said. It was the first time I'd ever heard him call her "Sugar" in the mean-spirited way everybody else did.

"Man, no way. What happened?" I asked.

He didn't answer. He just produced a joint and asked me if I would give him a ride.

We got high and drove around out in bumfuck trying to deliver a lousy quarter bag to an address we never could find. Given the atmosphere of the kudzu patches, we listened to the *Murmur* side of the R.E.M. tape. He sang out loud to "Radio Free Europe."

He had told me once before about how he'd spent an entire year of high school in his bedroom listening to that album, so I was shocked by how many of the lyrics he botched. Of course, the crowd around the Commune were making a myth with their little comments about him falling on his head and all the cartoonish impact that must have had on his intelligence. I hated to admit it, but I did wonder. But then he'd been saying and doing stupid shit the entire time I'd known him.

I managed to bust a tail light on a fence post while attempting a three-point turn in an anonymous gravel drive that was leading nowhere except into deep troughs of mud and even deeper weeds. I was too messed up to be driving, and Mickey's navigator skills were the worst I'd ever encountered. I pulled over to check out the damage and surrendered to a cigarette break. I left the ignition on so we could still have the music, and we sat on the hood with our feet on the bumper facing the pressing country darkness.

Cicadas, crickets, and frogs screamed relentlessly, like a skipping CD. Did they make all that racket hoping for rain? The faintest heat lightning flickered on the horizon, but it was that electric tease that never results in any dynamic weather. It was more of a taunting reminder that the air wasn't moving at all—that the temperature hadn't dropped a single degree since nightfall.

"So, you and Hutch," Mickey said, squinting into the distance like he was watching a TV off in a field, just on the other side of the barbed wire fence drowning in honeysuckle. "You guys were becoming, like, a couple. And then that dude he was into in high school—the one he swears isn't gay—called him up last minute and invited him to New York. And he just left?"

"Yep."

"You'd already rented a house."

"I put down a *deposit* on a house. Fortunately, I was able to get it back. They had someone else who wanted the place."

"Fuck, brother, I'm sorry. I had no idea Hutch could be such a dick."

I changed the subject by bringing up the breakup with Charlotte again.

"You know she's almost twenty-five years old, right?" He whispered it, like he was scandalized by it. Or like someone might possibly overhear him way out in the middle of nowhere. "She's been a dropout for over five years. I think she might have just made it through her freshman year, but beyond that, she's been lying to her parents about being in school ever since. Her dad makes a fuss about it, at least every once in a while. But apparently he always gives in at some point, and ends up putting more money in her account." He chuckled, remembering something, and shook his head in what could have been either disbelief or admiration. "She told them she completed a degree in biology with a 3.0 GPA. I guess she thought a solid low B wouldn't raise too many eyebrows, but it also wouldn't be too hard to explain why she didn't get into medical school later on. She must have come up with one hell of an elaborate excuse for missing her own supposed graduation ceremony *and* to convince them not to come to it. She bought herself some extended time in Athens by claiming she'd been accepted into some kind of x-ray tech graduate program or some bullshit like that. In reality, she told me she has less than twenty total credit hours, with, like, a 1.3 GPA."

So much for his rumored brain injury and inability to recall minute details. I murmured some agreement about how messed up it all was. "I went to school with a ton of spoiled motherfuckers," I said. "But I have to say, Charlotte's beyond any trust fund kid I've ever met. She's like the real-life inspiration for a Tennessee Williams play about a sorority girl, fallen from debutante glamor, crossed with, like, *Less Than Zero*." Good pot sometimes caused me to converse in random literary allusions, instead of the usual music associations.

Mickey bummed one of my cigarettes and smoked it in silence.

"You never really answered my question," I said.

"What question?"

"What happened with her? With Charlotte?"

"Brother, she beat the shit out of me."

"Last night?" I asked.

"No, like, pretty much the whole time we were together. Every other fucking day. Screaming, knock-down, drag-out fights. I mean, *physical* shit. I swear to God, though, I never started it. I never hit her back."

"What could have possibly pissed her off that much?" I wondered out loud.

He didn't hesitate to answer. "Money. Always fucking

money. It's what she fights with her dad about; it's what she fights with her mom about; it's what she fights with me about. It's all she talks about. Well, when nobody else is around. Like, when you came over, she's all New Age *Gone with the Wind* and shit."

"Man, I know that's totally put on. Everybody knows she's fake. That's why they make fun of her."

"She pushed me off the roof," he said.

"Are you *serious*?"

"Fuck, yeah, I'm serious. You've seen her do that thing with the clouds, right?"

I reluctantly nodded my head. "Twice."

"That's not fake. She's really... *doing* that. She can fucking control the weather. And, yes, before you ask, I thought that before I fell on my head."

I held up my hands in surrender. "I believe you."

"We were fighting, and she was yelling at me: calling me names and throwing shit at me across the apartment. I climbed out onto the roof, you know, to get away from her. When I got to the other end of the building, there was this gust of wind that came up out of nowhere. It didn't push me, it literally fucking *dragged* me off the roof. I was hanging on to the gutter and it was like a 250-pound man had me by the ankles. Pulling me toward the ground. The whole time, I could hear her cussing me, like she was right there beside me. She was still in her apartment, but I could hear every word she said, like she was right there in my ear. I eventually lost my grip."

"Holy shit," I said. "But she drove you to the hospital, right?"

"Hell, no, she didn't drive me to the hospital. I just got up and started walking away from there, fast as I could. I was a couple of blocks down Milledge, and some guys I know were driving by and recognized me. They saw blood all over my face and drove me to the emergency room."

"She called me at home and told me *she* took you to the emergency room," I said.

"That's laughable. She doesn't drive. She has a car, but she's afraid to get in it. She doesn't even leave her apartment."

"Ever?" I asked.

"Never."

He went silent again for a few minutes and then out of nowhere said, "I did slap her."

He turned to read a bunch of questions off my raised eyebrows.

"Last night," he said. "I finally lost it. I hit her back. It wasn't a slap, actually; that's a lie too. It was more of a punch."

I didn't so much say "And?" as I prompted him with a full-body gesture.

"I don't even...." He spread his hands, looked up, and held his open palms out like maybe some words would fall out of the sky. "I can't." He sighed, dropped his chin to his chest, pushed his bowler hat off his head, and ran his hands through his hair. He stared at the ground.

I put my arm around his shoulders and squeezed him in an awkward kind of sideways hug. We stayed like that, neither of us saying anything. He smelled like a campfire. Like really sweaty clothes worn near a campfire in the rain.

And his mouth reeked of tobacco when—I didn't see it coming—he turned toward me and kissed me.

It was a clumsy kiss, but not hesitant. He must have decided and acted in the moment. I messed up his landing by initially pulling away before realizing, in the same split second, that it might hurt his feelings. I received it holding my breath, thinking surely this was some weird expression of affection or gratitude—definitely not anything sexual.

Then he repositioned his lips, parted them slightly, and came at me for *another* one.

This time I pulled away. "Dude, what are you doing? You're not gay." He looked so embarrassed. I tried to save him by making a joke out of it. "Damn, how high *are* you?" I forced a laugh.

He went along with that, jumped down off the hood of the car, grabbed his hat from the gravel, and shook his head as if he was trying to clear it. "That's some good shit, huh?"

I felt bad for him. He didn't say anything on the drive home, so I rattled on, babbling about the daydreams I had of Hutch showing up on my doorstep, what I would say to him, the various lines I'd rehearsed...I didn't even know how much I had been doing that until I started confessing it. I'm sure it sounded pathetic. I wouldn't have wanted anybody to know how much I thought about Hutch, but I desperately needed to make sure Mickey knew he was still my friend. That I wasn't mad or bothered about the kiss.

I mean, I didn't *care*, although I was kind of weirded out by it. There had never been any indication that Mickey was interested in guys in general, or me in particular.

When I pulled into the driveway between the cottage and his house and stopped near the door into the basement where he stayed, he finally spoke. He said he was thinking he should go back over to Charlotte's and try to talk to her.

"Man, I don't think that's a good idea," I said.

"Maybe if I apologize," he said, "and try to work things out, she'll stay."

"Mickey, I don't think her leaving has that much to do with you."

He nodded, looking defeated, and stared at the floorboard with his arm on the door handle. And then he asked me if he could borrow some money. God bless him, he genuinely believed I "came from wealth."

Instead of telling him no, I told him why. "Listen. This car is a piece of shit. And it's not a hand-me-down from my parents. I worked my ass off to buy it even though my dad begged me not to waste my money on it. It's way too expensive to fix. There's no telling what that tail light is going to cost. The only people who can afford to drive a Mercedes drive a new one. Mine is all just for show, man."

I trailed off, staring at him, hoping he could do the math. He met my eyes for a moment but quickly glanced away from whatever he saw there.

"I gotcha, brother," he said. "It's cool." He rolled out of the car, and without ever standing fully upright, disappeared down the stairwell like it was a plain old hole in the ground.

EIGHT

On Friday, the phone in the cottage rang for the second time. The sound was still a surreal combination of commonplace and completely unusual. I thought, *Yes, finally, it's Hutch.*

It was Agent Wood.

"Mr. Stewart!" He sounded excited to speak with me. "Good afternoon. Got a quick question for ya."

How in the hell did he know to call me here? Later, it dawned on me that the phone was in my name. In that moment of panic, I just stupidly tried to match his friendliness. "Okay, shoot"—the worst possible word choice. "What do you need to know?"

"I need to know where I can find Malcolm Walker," he said.

"Who?"

"Your friend, Mickey." I could hear him shuffling

papers. "Now, this campus address from last year...of course, that's no good. I know he was spending a lot of time at your friend Charlotte's, but she says they've broken up. You know where else I might track him down?"

"Um..." Was it possible he could tell over the phone that I was suddenly nauseous?

"He's not there with you right now, is he?" His tone pretended I was an incorrigible prankster.

"No," I said. "I just moved in. Nobody's been here but me."

"All right. Well, I won't keep you then," he said, almost like he was politely apologizing for calling the wrong number. "I'll track him down eventually."

When I hung up the phone I realized I didn't feel sick as much as guilty: deep down, I was praying that Agent Wood would find Mickey so that he'd stop calling me.

NINE

On Saturday afternoon, Gavin picked me up and drove me to the party at his fraternity. He was still wearing out that cassette of *The Joshua Tree*. I was relieved to find him dressed pretty much like all the guys I'd known in high school: high-water khakis, a yellow Oxford shirt with a navy jacket, and shitty-looking docksides. No socks, thank God. I wore a more well-pressed version of the same uniform, only with a sky-blue shirt that went better with my coloring and navy-paneled, lace-up saddle Oxfords that took the whole preppy statement to a new level of garish sarcasm.

It was a mostly predictable gathering in a Georgian revival mansion that screamed Twelve Oaks from the outside—assuming you overlooked the red plastic Solo cups that were already collecting along the front steps. The inside was cleared of furniture in a way that made it feel like it had been abandoned by its owners just before being overtaken by a crush of drunk guys in blue blazers.

There were woefully fewer females than even my most conservative suspicions might have predicted.

The music bordered on sacrilegious for Athens: Drivin' 'N' Cryin', some INXS, and more Drivin' 'N' Cryin'. A couple of token tracks from R.E.M.'s *Lifes Rich Pageant* dug the mainstream trench that much deeper.

Gavin pinched the cuff of my sleeve and dragged me in his wake through the crowd. I don't think anyone noticed, but my face betrayed me with a flush. No one stopped us to speak to him, but he lifted his chin in acknowledgement of a few people far across the sea of heads.

We made our way to the smaller back porch set up with the beer kegs. Some guy with a bowl cut was pouring what was probably yet another full bottle of pure grain alcohol into a black plastic trashcan of hunch punch.

"The punch, definitely," Gavin said. He used his fingers to tweeze out the cup floating among the chunks of fruit, ladled out two tall portions of grapefruit-pink liquid, and handed one to me. "A decent buzz without having to fight our way back over here again and again. Cool?"

I didn't remember if I'd told Gavin that I didn't drink. I couldn't think of how it would have come up. I'm not sure why I spontaneously decided to make an exception, but I said, "Fine with me. Cheers." I banged my cup against the side of Gavin's and sipped the tiniest bit. It was like fruit-scented kerosene. The second swallow was easier. I gulped a few mouthfuls while my taste buds were still in shock.

A girl beside us shrieked. "A tornado watch? Oh, my God, for real?" she asked her friend. "Isn't it kind of like the wrong time of year or something?"

I peered up at the patch of sky visible through gaps in the tree canopy. It was overcast and silvery green.

"I hate lightning," her friend said.

I rolled my eyes at Gavin. "Let's get away from them, please," I said, without moving my lips.

"Follow me." This time he reached for my hand and squeezed it, holding on to my thumb for a few seconds before eventually sliding back up to my sleeve. I resisted the urge to yank it away. It did make it easier to follow him through the crowd.

We positioned ourselves in the front room beside the fireplace at one end of a deep bay window. Gavin held brief, banal conversations with people as they passed through the front door and merged into the slow-moving front of bodies sliding toward the alcohol at the back of the house. He introduced me by my first name, as you might anyone, and they all smiled and shook my hand before scudding on.

Then I heard him say, "This is Rusty. My *date*."

Whoever the guy was, Bill Somebody, laughed and slapped Gavin on the arm. He also pumped my hand, flashed perfect teeth, said "Nice to meet you," and just moved on.

Gavin turned to me with a face of exaggerated incredulity. "He didn't even flinch!"

"He probably thought you were joking," I said, irritated.

Gavin didn't seem to note the tone of my voice. He leaned in close to my ear and nodded toward the straight couple making out beside us. "What if I just started kissing you like that, right here, right now?" Even though he yelled it, no one would have heard him over the background of party noise.

I pushed him away. He grinned like he thought I was teasing. I wasn't. "Man, we talked about this. I told you I don't want to be a part of some scene, just so you can have a big coming-out moment with your brothers here."

He laughed nervously. "Ah, gee, come on. Why not?"

I raised my eyebrows at him with a look I hoped was significantly withering.

His face suddenly fell. "You're not embarrassed for people to know you're with me, are you?"

"What? No! Absolutely not." I vehemently shook my head, frowning as sincerely as possible. "That is not it at all. But if you want to be with me, in public, you know really *be* with me, and be yourself...there's somewhere better we can go."

"Where?" he sniggered. "A parking lot?"

"No, asshole. Another party."

"Like, a *gay* party?"

I shrugged and rolled my eyes. "Well, yeah."

He proceeded to ask a bunch of naïve, gratuitous questions about what I meant, exactly, by a "gay" party.

I think I did a fairly good job of realistically forecasting the atmosphere we'd find there. In other words, lowering his expectations. "It's not an orgy, okay? It's just a party. Most of the people there will be gay or gay-friendly or just cool. Or whatever. The point is, they certainly won't care that you are."

"Well, hell yeah. Let's go, before I'm too drunk to drive."

"You're already too drunk to drive. But it's only about six or seven blocks. We can walk."

Outside, after getting snagged by a few good-byes, he caught up with me on the sidewalk and asked, "Where to?"

"Very close to our special spot." I grimaced.

"No way." Of course he knew exactly where I meant, but he seemed genuinely amused by it.

"Yep. Right across the street. Corner of Milledge Terrace and Castalia."

It was way too hot and humid to be wearing blazers. The stumps that Charlotte had described, the enormous old oaks that had been pulled down by storms, were that much more noticeable on foot.

As we walked, Gavin interviewed me about the details of how, when, and where I "came out of the closet." I swear to God, his words came straight out of a high school guidance counselor's pamphlet on teen sexuality.

"I wasn't really ever 'in the closet' much past junior high," I said. It annoyed me that I couldn't help but whisper when I used expressions like that. I glanced over my shoulder, even though I knew there was no one close to us. I read somewhere one time that Scorpios often have a persistent sense that they're being followed, watched, spied upon, or videotaped. "I wanted to get laid, just like any other guy. I even wanted to date. I refused to miss out on that just because a bunch of straight assholes wanted to make me feel like I had to hide."

"You didn't get harassed?" Gavin asked, his eyes on the uneven sidewalk that unrolled under his weaving footsteps.

"I cultivated an aura of barely contained rage, violence, and potential insanity," I said, watching for the occasional tree root that broke through the blocks of pavement. "If you called me a faggot, I punched the shit out of you before the slur was even off your lips. In seventh grade, when I was still going to public school, this kid called me a fag in front of my whole gym class. The coach didn't even say anything to him. So I kicked the kid in the nuts as hard as I could. When he hit the ground, I kicked him in the gut a couple of times. I was aiming for his face when they pulled me off of him. Nobody bothered me for a long time after that."

"Fuck!" Gavin said, stumbling into me. "You just *did* that?"

I held on to his elbow while he regained his balance. "When I was in second grade, this older boy, a fifth grader, was messing with me at the bus stop every morning. I'd come home and whine to my mom about it. She kept telling me if I hauled off and punched him in the nose, he'd leave me alone. Well, I put up with it for several more days. I don't know, maybe a week. And finally, I'd just had it. I popped the shit out of him. His nose bled like hell. It scared me as much as it did him or anybody who saw it. But after I calmed down, I realized that it worked. You should've seen the way he acted after that. He wouldn't even make eye contact with me. It was like someone had given me a secret magical power. I wanted to do it again. Not long after that, my parents ended up putting me in boxing lessons because they thought I was becoming too aggressive. Watch out—"

I jerked Gavin to a stop by the collar of his jacket as a car pulled onto the side street in front of us.

"So, you actually know how to fight, like, for real," he said, swaying worse standing still than he had while walking.

"Let's cross now," I said, making sure that we both safely negotiated the curbs before I continued my story. "In eighth grade, this football player—big guy—started body-slamming me whenever he passed me in the hall. That was back before they used to automatically suspend both people for fighting, regardless of who started it or whose fault it was. But I did have a warning in my file because of the incident in gym. Anyway, so I sharpened a pencil and walked with it under my armpit, just like I had my arms crossed around my books. I didn't have to do anything. When he rammed into me, he impaled himself on the pencil. He made a big scene. He didn't bleed that much or anything, but he yelled and carried on. Luckily, he was fat enough that it didn't puncture his lung. And the algebra teacher came to my defense. She'd seen him doing it, every day like clockwork. Same time, same place, in the hall right in front of her room. The teachers knew I was being bullied. They knew why. I made good grades. They liked me. They did not like the kids I usually got into it with. I'm pretty sure more than a few of them, including the vice-principal, were secretly cheering me on, wishing they could do it themselves."

"Bad *ass*," Gavin said, winding up to kick a pebble and not even realizing it when he missed.

"My mom got me into private school in ninth grade. And somehow my reputation followed me there." I was a little breathless from all the talking, walking, and alcohol. "It was a lot better after that."

"You really *weren't* worried about getting harassed back there at Theta Chi." Gavin turned around to face me and started walking backward. "You were afraid you'd go off and fuck somebody up, weren't you?"

"Being bullied doesn't intimidate me, or scare me. It pisses me the fuck off. I refuse to be just another sissy who takes shit off people."

"I think that's hot," he said, grinning and wagging his eyebrows at me before thankfully falling back into step beside me.

"You know, man, I just expected everybody else to be out once I got to college," I said, offering the palms of my hands to the whole town around us and looking up at the hacked-open crowns of the crape myrtles that had been trimmed back from the power lines. "I meet all these guys who I know are gay, and they know I'm fully out about it, and they don't have a problem with it. But they still act like they don't know what they want. What the hell is taking y'all so long?"

When we took a right at Milledge Circle, there was a U-Haul pulled up on the sidewalk in front of Charlotte's building. The street-level door was propped open with a brick. I could see that the French doors were open to her porch and the lamp on the credenza was still on. I wondered if Mickey had gone back by there. Who else would she get to help her move?

I slowed down as we approached a house with people crowding the front porch and the strains of classic B-52s pouring out the open door and windows. "This is it," I said.

"Who lives here?" Gavin asked.

"You'll probably recognize them. A couple of the dandies who hang out in the square in front of Cookies & Company Café. The ones with their own table. They're always there."

"Oh, yeah, I've seen those guys. One of them's handsome, like in a GQ model kind of way. Blond? Wears his hair in a ponytail tied with a ribbon, like it's 1776 or some shit?"

"That's Aaron. He really is a model. He was in a Benetton ad. He's a manager at the Gap. I tried to get a job there, but he turned me down. He's actually pretty cool, though; he's the one who invited me." I realized we were being stared at. "Come on, everybody's wondering why the hell we're just standing out here by the mailbox."

I don't know that I felt much more comfortable at this party than I did at the other. The music was definitely better. People were dressed cooler. I felt ridiculously self-conscious that Gavin and I were wearing what basically amounted to matching school uniforms. We'd been almost invisible at the frat house, our clothes acting as camouflage. Here, it felt like we were the only ones who had shown up in costume.

Gavin held on to my sleeve again, only this time I led the way through the crowd toward whatever alcohol would inevitably be found at the back of the house.

A few people openly gaped at us. I'm pretty sure I saw an eye roll. A knot of guys twittered to one another and burst into cackles just as we walked past. It was impossible not to assume they were laughing at us.

No one spoke to me.

I mean, I saw a lot of familiar faces, but not really anyone I could technically call a "close" friend. A highly recognizable guy from a heavy-rotation MTV video elbowed past us. I glanced over my shoulder at Gavin. Ironically, he was trying too hard to check everyone out, without looking like he was, to have noticed the local celebrity. He raised his eyebrows at me, but I'm not sure what the expression was intended to convey. His cheeks were flushed; he looked kind of terrified.

I found Aaron in the kitchen, holding court around an island. I introduced Gavin to him, and Aaron introduced us both to everyone standing within his immediate circle of conversation. He broke away from them and pointed us toward the keg in an empty breakfast nook. Gavin and I both made appropriate comments about the house being cool.

Aaron glanced down at our clothes and then tactfully asked if we'd gone to another "event." When I told him we'd just come from a fraternity party, he confessed that he was intrigued. For some reason, I found myself volunteering the part about Gavin taking me as his date.

"That's brave," Aaron said to Gavin, seeming genuinely impressed. "What did your frat brothers think of that?"

Gavin looked embarrassed but pleased by the direct attention. "Um..." He turned to me for corroboration. "They didn't even really seem to notice, did they?"

"Honestly, it was kind of anticlimactic," I told Aaron. "But I didn't think we should push the gay rights agenda, so we headed over here."

Aaron nodded knowingly, graciously welcomed us, and told us to enjoy ourselves.

A white guy with blond dreadlocks and eyes like a wolf pumped beers for us from the keg. We thanked him for the pair of red plastic cups—as ubiquitous here as at the previous engagement—and wandered back through the house the way we'd come.

"Everybody's really nice," Gavin said. "Aaron seems cool."

"So, I guess you're good to stay then?"

"Yeah, definitely." He took a swig of his beer, licked the foam off his lip, and grinned. I just held my cup as a kind of theatrical prop.

A lot of people were checking us out. They'd all seen me plenty of times, so of course they were more interested in Gavin. Most of the men I knew would probably not have liked to admit it, but straight guys, bisexuals, closet cases—even other gays, when they're new—they were all blood in the water to a whole streak of hunters who preferred stranger prey. Gavin was also better looking than ninety-nine percent of the guys there. If only we'd brought a change of clothes, I wouldn't have minded being seen with him even the little bit that I did.

We loitered in the hallway in line for the only bathroom. When it was Gavin's turn he asked me if I wanted to come in with him.

"Why, you think I'm going to hold it for you?"

"You can if you want to," he said. His breath smelled like warm beer and the sour fruit punch from earlier.

It was not good protocol for couples to disappear into a bathroom together at a crowded house party and start groping each other when there were people legitimately needing to piss. Doors would be banged on. There would be an angry gauntlet of annoyed people with their arms folded when we got out. No way.

I rolled my eyes and pushed him inside on his own. "Hurry," I told him.

He was mercifully quick. After trading places with me, he said he was going to get another beer and wait for me out on the back deck.

I peed and then checked my hair, teeth, and nose in the mirror over the sink. I wondered why Gavin seemed to be such a glutton for shame.

When I came out, I pushed my way back through the living and dining rooms, waiting patiently as the crowd shifted by unhurried inches. I was almost out the back door when I got stuck in the kitchen, unable to get around a ring of people talking by the keg. I was standing directly behind a spark plug of a guy who had chosen to hide his early male pattern baldness by shaving his head. Probably the best spin on virile beauty he could hope for. He was squat and muscular, with a bristly five o'clock shadow, but when he spoke he sounded like a girl.

All his friends were leaning to peer openly through the back screen door. He was clearly talking about somebody out on the deck. "I mean, is that like a dress code or something?"

"I know, right?" said an elfin character wearing eyeliner. "Their little outfits *match*."

"Fucking frat boy closet cases, slumming at the townie fag party."

They all erupted in a chorus of vicious giggles. They were talking about Gavin. They were talking about us.

One of them saw me. I made eye contact. "Come on, you guys." he said, flushing. "Aaron invited them."

I leaned in close to the ear of the muscular one who'd just called me a closet case. He stank of patchouli. A hippie with no hair. *Please.* "Who the fuck are you talking about?" I asked quietly. Not a whisper, but that kind of evil, low tone that hides a cruel smile within it.

He whirled around, visibly flustered to find me right on top of him. The recognition in his eyes was impossible to hide. The shadow of an impulse to apologize passed across his features.

"Who the *fuck* are you talking about?" I repeated through clenched teeth.

He probably bantered about all kinds of bitchy responses with these queens on a daily basis, always quick with a cutting word. But now he chose a silent look of smug admission with a meaningfully arched eyebrow. He deliberately looked me up and down with a moue of disgust, and then, without deigning to answer, turned his back on me.

I heard his dismissive exhale. He must have rolled his eyes again or mouthed something to his group because most of them laughed.

And that did it for me.

Before either of us realized it was actually happening, I spun him around to face me. Balling the collar of his shirt in my fist and jamming it under his chin, I forced his head up and his mouth closed. I heard—and felt—his teeth clack together.

I drove him through the screen door, slamming it open and ignoring the sudden shouts from all around us.

I shoved the little prick toward Gavin.

"Apologize!" I screamed.

My voice left my body and fled across the grass in a spreading ripple. Plastic cups tumbled off the deck railing in a rain of deep, ping pong ball tones. Several people on the deck fled down the steps into the yard. The sudden sound of ocean waves in the roiling leaves overhead drew everyone's attention toward the yellowing sky. Some tried to shield their eyes from the dust, wind-whipped hair, and thousands of twig spears and curled brown arrows torn from the treetops.

"Apologize!" It tore from my throat, more of a bellow this time. A roar.

"No!" he spat. His voice sounded thick. I was pretty sure he'd bitten his tongue. His face was bright red. He acted petulant, but I could tell he was scared.

I lunged toward him. He attempted a clumsy karate move, almost as if to hold me away from him with his foot. The kick wasn't high enough. It landed against the top of my thigh. I grabbed his ankle and twisted his leg; the maneuver forced him into a cartwheel, his hands scrabbling over splinters in the rough boards.

Holding on to his foot, I leaned backward with all my weight and started dragging him as fast as I could.

He tried to keep up, crab-walking on his elbows. When I reached the edge of the porch near the opening for the stairs, I changed direction and drove him like a wheelbarrow.

And dumped him headfirst off the deck.

I stood looking down at him for one silent second. A bolt of fear shot through me, that I might have killed him. A crowd of people descended on him, blocking him from my view.

One face turned up toward me, purple with rage. "Get him out of here!"

Even though I could see the veins in the forehead—the tendons standing out along his throat were evidence of just how loudly he shouted at me—it sounded like it was coming through earplugs. Through a pillow. From far away. The aftermath of adrenaline.

I was grabbed by the shoulders and pulled back from the railing. It was Gavin, embracing me, lifting me slightly off my feet, like a wrestling hold. I couldn't hear anything but my own breathing and a roaring-like wind in my ears.

I was shoved, sucked, yanked, and carried through a vortex of faces, some disgusted, some smirking. More than most of them just looked like they were wondering what the fuck was going on.

Once back out on the front porch, Gavin took me by the elbow and dragged me along the path of paving stones to the street. Dried leaves skittered in an invisible stream against the curb along the sidewalk. I tripped as we joined them, momentum making it difficult to keep my footing.

Gavin pushed me back in the direction from where we'd come earlier. A river of air above our heads rushed through the tops of the crape myrtles and dogwoods that lined both sides of Milledge Terrace.

Behind us, people exited the house, a knot of four or five guys expelled faster than the others, squinting and angry. The one I'd thrown off the porch screamed for us to stop, his friends pulling at his arms to restrain him. I must not have hurt the guy too badly. At least two others advanced toward us.

The sky had turned a flat and silver color, like the underside of flapping summer maple leaves. Across the street and up the drive, I caught a glimpse of a patrol car parked in the lot behind Charlotte's building—in the space-that-wasn't-a-space by the Dumpster.

"Stop stop stop stop stop slow *down!*" I hissed at Gavin. "Walk normal."

"What?" He stumbled as he tried to look around to see what I was reacting to. "They're still following us."

"There's a cop *right there*," I said. "You know it's probably Brody."

Gavin's head whipped around and then back to me. "Shit!" He fell into a pace of forced calm alongside me, his eyes unfocused on the ground in front of his feet, his hands shoved into his jacket pockets. But then he suddenly stopped, bent over, and leaned on his thighs.

"What are you doing?" I whined. "Keep walking."

He mumbled something and staggered over to a hedge covered in clematis. "I gotta puke."

"Aw, come on, man. Not here."

"I can't..." He couldn't. I heard him making gagging noises.

Two of the three guys following us had stopped and were watching the other one head straight for the lot where the patrol car was parked. No doubt to enlist the officer in apprehending us.

The U-Haul was directly opposite us, pulled up on the sidewalk closest to the door that led to Charlotte's apartment. If I could get us to the far side of the truck, we wouldn't be out in the open. As far as anybody walking down the street was concerned, we would basically disappear.

"Cross!" I barked at Gavin. I lifted him under the armpits, as he'd done with me, and half-carried him to the side of Charlotte's building.

He staggered the rest of the way up into the small wedge of park that fronted the street entrance. The spread of the magnolia's branches formed a hollow interior space large enough to conceal us, even while standing comfortably upright. I pushed him through the outer layer of clattering leaves and followed him inside. He hung on to a ladder of branches and retched onto the surprisingly bare ground.

I hoped all the noise he was making was absorbed by the rising wind.

Then I saw Officer Brody. He and another cop were moving right toward the tree where we were hiding. They were walking as fast as they could without jogging. I could hear the jangling of the equipment on their belts.

They bore down on top of us.

But at the last possible second, they turned right and dove into the building's entrance. I heard the scrape of the brick that propped the door open, the boom as it slammed shut, and the pounding of their boots echoing up the stairs to Charlotte's door.

They weren't after us.

Breathing hard and ignoring Gavin's moaning and spitting, I closed my eyes and sank into a flood of relief.

And then sirens began to wail.

My first panicked thought was *squad cars.* For just a second there, I thought we were surrounded. But the sound was bigger, more haunting than urgent. It seemed to come from far away across town and from every direction all at once. Like an air raid warning from a documentary with gritty footage of the Blitz.

It was a tornado warning siren.

Everybody has seen a dervish whirl into being in the dead-end brick corner of an alley, or a dust devil spin up into a hanging sculpture of leaves above a patch of asphalt. Those manifestations are nearly human in size and usually rooted to the ground. This vortex unfurled forty feet in the air, a fold in the fabric of space above the treetops. It would have been invisible had it not shaken open a cloak of debris and draped itself in a fabric of cigarette butts and paper trash. The leaves of a crape myrtle took flight like birds from bare winter branches seen from a distance. They coalesced at the maelstrom's center like a cartoon hornet swarm belched from its nest in reverse.

I didn't duck or lie low. The thought of crouching never even occurred to me. Instead of instinctive fear, I felt only power, uplifted and compelled to stretch tall on my toes.

The gray current wrapped itself around a tree a few hundred yards away, an enormous bolt of wet gauze that hung limp among the branches, and then, with a mighty upward yank, tore away the bulk of the tree's mass. Only a few feet of the bole remained above an enormous tilted scab of dirt and roots.

I screamed my throat hoarse. I cheered as the giant ghost twirled away down Milledge Avenue, crashing into one tree, swinging around another, and randomly kicking parked cars onto their sides.

I'd never witnessed anything like it: a ballet of rage, the walking fingertips of chaos, the blind whims of weather. It was gone in a minute. I had to believe it was magic. And I had good reason to hope it was mine.

Or maybe it was hers.

I looked up at Charlotte's. From that steep angle,

directly below, I could detect only the shadows of frantic movement thrown onto the ceiling above her porch. In the weird gloom, I could tell that the lamp on her credenza was still on.

The street-level door slung open.

Someone stumbled out onto the stoop and fell on all fours. A black bowler hat went rolling into the mulch. Mickey struggled to stand, the skin on his bare knees scraped white from sliding across the concrete but still too shocked to bleed. I opened my mouth to call out to him, but before I could form a word, Officer Brody appeared and tackled him flat. With a knee on Mickey's back, he cuffed his hands. His partner joined him, and together they jerked Mickey up by his elbows and dragged him away down the sidewalk.

We waited a few minutes beneath the magnolia, in case the cops came back. Gavin dozed a bit, sitting on the ground at the base of the tree, his chin drooping progressively toward his chest. He jerked awake a couple of times to complain that he was thirsty.

It wasn't long before I saw the patrol car speed away. Apparently, no one had followed us over from the scene I'd caused at the party either.

I kept expecting Charlotte to come downstairs. I finally moved Gavin out onto the stoop so that no one would come along and find him passed out in the bushes. I propped him up in a relatively normal position, elbows on knees, and promised to bring him back a cup of water if I could. I went up to pound on Charlotte's door.

No answer. There was never any sign of her.

"Come on," I said, grabbing Gavin by the hands and pulling him to his feet. "We can get you a Gatorade from the convenience store."

Following the path of the storm, Gavin and I walked back down Milledge Avenue to the Theta Chi house where we'd left his car. Neither of us said anything the entire way. Gavin was fully occupied with trying to drink and walk at the same time, every jarring misstep causing him to grunt like he'd just been punched in the stomach. I felt ecstatic, something more like an exercise high than any buzz I was used to having. My eyes were drawn toward the sky, scanning for more phenomena in the treetops. There I noticed winks of light, like the sparkles you see in the clouds from an airplane window.

Gavin was clearly too wasted to drive me anywhere. His frat brothers promised to see that he slept it off. I felt mostly relieved to hand him back over. They showed me where I could use the phone, which I used to call my new roommate Alexandra and ask her to pick me up.

By the time we turned onto South Lumpkin on the way home, Charlotte's apartment was dark. The lamp on the credenza by the French doors was turned off; the U-Haul had vanished.

She was gone.

When we pulled up to the cottage, I told Alexandra that I needed to get something out of my car. While she unlocked the front door and went inside, I fumbled open my trunk. I pulled the ribbon off Charlotte's gift and folded aside the layers of tissue. There lay her papa's velvet smoking jacket and her nana's flapper beads; they had been making the rattle in the bottom of the box.

I hadn't really thought of Charlotte as a friend, but she apparently had thought of me as one.

TEN

The next day, I saw TJ/CJ out in the yard behind the Commune. He told me that he and the other roommates didn't want Mickey living there anymore, and that, when Mickey heard about it, he said he didn't want anyone to bother bailing him out of jail if he didn't have anywhere to stay.

"I feel bad," I said to Alexandra. "I want to be that friend that runs to rescue him, no questions asked. But there's no room for him here. There's barely enough room for *me*." Alexandra had taken the closet-sized bedroom; Gabrielle's futon and stereo were tucked into the sunroom off the kitchen; and my personal space was technically the cottage's living room.

"Does that even matter?" Alexandra asked. "I mean, you can't pay his bail."

She had no way of knowing that the money didn't matter, either. That the last thing I wanted to do was connect myself to Mickey's legal troubles by voluntarily going anywhere near a police station. She mistook my grimace of guilt and self-preservation as genuine regret and empathy.

"Honey, don't worry about it," she said. "I'm sure his parents are taking care of everything."

That did seem like the most likely thing to happen, and not just because I wanted to believe so.

I braced myself every time the phone rang, expecting some new string of foreboding calls. I'd all but completely forgotten my fantasies of what I would say when I finally heard Hutch's voice on the other end of the line. Now the bad TV scripts in my head included a summons to appear in court to testify against Mickey. (Is that even something they would call you on the phone about, or would they send you a letter?) Or some lawyer his parents had hired wanting me to make a statement, to interview me as a potential witness for the defense.

I wondered if Charlotte would be dragged back to town. She'd probably give some performance, and her delusional shit would sound more convincing than any truth I'd sworn to tell.

And then I thought, *Oh, God, what if I have to sit through that frat boy getting grilled on the stand about having sex in my car?*

For a few weeks, I expected to run into Gavin, at least coming out of the Commune next door. I assumed that after being introduced to the townie side of Athens he'd start popping up everywhere I went. But it was pretty much like he'd never even existed. I didn't really care if I saw him—I just preferred to have some warning.

I hadn't actually heard anything to make me think that any of the anxious fictions I'd invented would ever become reality. But it was best for me if they all stayed where they'd been put.

The Sunday before classes started, I came home from the University Bookstore to find Alexandra waiting for me with a funny look on her face.

"What?" I asked.

She arched her right eyebrow. "We had a call."

Oh, shit. "Yeah..."

Her head leaned to one side and her mouth twitched with a small, bitter smile. "Hutch," she said. That funny look was pity. She felt sorry for me.

Feigning annoyance, I rolled my eyes, sighed, and dropped the bag of textbooks to the floor. The bang was louder than intended; Alexandra jumped.

"I didn't talk to him," she rushed to tell me. "Gabrielle was the only one here when he called."

I flapped my arms against my sides in genuine disgust. "Of course. Great." Gabrielle had spent the last half of freshman year trying to date Hutch, while he was fooling around with me in our dorm room every time he came home with a buzz.

"Hutch *did* tell her that he'd spoken to Mickey's parents. Mickey's dad drove up to get him out of jail and took him back home to South Georgia. He probably won't be back any time soon. Not this quarter anyway."

In the mornings, when I drove through the Five Points intersection on my way to campus, or at night on my way home from the bars, I looked up at Charlotte's screened porch. Her credenza light, and the particular shadows it cast, never came back. Eventually there were signs of a new occupant: new lights, new window coverings, new movements. Once, when I was walking out of the Bottle Shop, I heard Guns N' Roses' "Sweet Child o' Mine" wailing from the open kitchen window.

I knew that summer had truly ended the day I realized that all the broken trees had either been sawed off or removed. I drove down Milledge Avenue, past the fresh stumps, listening to The Smiths' *Meat Is Murder*. There were several places where the sidewalk blocks remained slightly buckled and would probably stay that way for decades. "Well I Wonder" was playing as I passed Charlotte's. I pulled up to the cottage before the song ended, so I sat in the driveway and waited for it to finish. Something about the quiet sound of the rain at the end of that track filled me with an unidentifiable sense of nostalgia.

Like I was already living in my own past.

ACKNOWLEDGMENTS

I owe a debt of gratitude to the beta readers who responded to early drafts: Kerry Vail, whose enthusiasm and validation encouraged me at a crucial moment; Charles Flatt, whose intelligence and criticism elevated my own perception of the work; Jewels Jones, whose mind for language and great taste in fiction made her wanting to read my story an incredible compliment.

To my editor, John Michael Arnaud, whose knowledge, talent, and skill blessed my project and made it better.

To Lacy Seale and Rebecca Feldbin, for moral support and for listening to me talk about the book (a lot).

To my parents, Sharon Roberson and James Roberson, for always believing that "a writer" was a perfectly valid answer to the question "What do you want to be when you grow up?"

ABOUT THE AUTHOR

Slade Roberson is a writer, professional intuitive counselor, and author of the highly regarded alternative spirituality blog *Shift Your Spirits*. He holds a degree in English from the University of Georgia and lives in Chattanooga, Tennessee. *Cloudbusting* is his first published novel.

www.sladeroberson.com

Made in the USA
Lexington, KY
03 April 2014